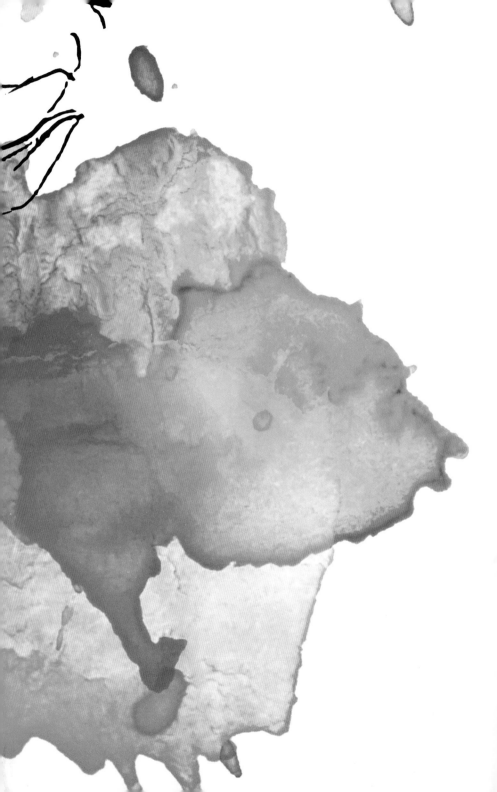

CHLOE *by* DESIGN

Measuring Up

BY MARGARET GUREVICH

ILLUSTRATIONS BY BROOKE HAGEL

Capstone Young Readers
a capstone imprint

Chloe by Design is published by Capstone Young Readers
A Capstone Imprint
1710 Roe Crest Drive
North Mankato, MN 56003
www.mycapstone.com

Text and illustrations © 2016 Capstone Young Readers

Library of Congress Cataloging-in-Publication Data

Names: Gurevich, Margaret, author. | Hagel, Brooke, illustrator. |
Gurevich, Margaret. Chloe by design.
Title: Chloe by design : measuring up / by Margaret Gurevich ;
illustrations by Brooke Hagel. Other titles: Measuring up
Description: North Mankato, Minnesota : Capstone Young Readers,
a Capstone imprint, [2016] | Series: Chloe by design | Summary: In
this compilation of four separately published books, Chloe is back in
Santa Cruz for her senior year in high school, facing the challenge of
reconnecting with her old friends (and rivals), and that most troublesome
problem of all — where to apply to college.
Identifiers: LCCN 2016003426| ISBN 9781623707279 (paper over board) |
ISBN 9781623707293 (ebook) | ISBN 9781623707286 (ebook pdf)
Subjects: LCSH: Fashion design--Juvenile fiction. | High school
seniors--Juvenile fiction. | College applications--Juvenile fiction. | Best
friends--Juvenile fiction. | Friendship--Juvenile fiction. |Santa Cruz
(Calif.)--Juvenile fiction. | CYAC: Fashion design--Fiction. |
High schools--Fiction. | Schools--Fiction. | College applications--
Fiction.| Best friends--Fiction. | Friendship--Fiction. | Santa Cruz
(Calif.)--Fiction.
Classification: LCC PZ7.G98146 Cj 2016 | DDC 813.6--dc23
LC record available at http://lccn.loc.gov/2016003426

Designer: Alison Thiele
Editor: Alison Deering

Artistic Elements: Shutterstock

Printed in China.
010031R

Measure twice, cut once
or you won't make the cut.

Dear Diary,

This past summer was too amazing for words! Interning for Stefan Meyers in New York City was such an incredible experience. I learned so much about the fashion industry during my eight weeks there. I used to think it was all about designing, but there's so much more to it than that. I know that designing is still what I want to do, but when I have my own label one day, it'll be good that I learned the behind-the-scenes stuff too.

The only disappointing thing about the summer was that I didn't get to see nearly as much of Jake — my sort-of friend, sort-of boyfriend — as I'd planned. I thought once I was in NYC we'd see each other all the time, since that's where he lives and goes to school. But being a working girl is a lot of pressure. We're still friends and stay in touch, but now that I'm back home in Cali we see each other even less. (I know there's nothing I can do about it, but it's hard not to feel a little left out when I see my best friend Alex and her new boyfriend, Dan.)

Speaking of feeling left out . . . I've been back home for almost a month now, and I still can't seem to get back into the groove. I feel miles away from everyone else, even Alex. Everyone is talking about college this and college that, and

I'm still adjusting to being back. People seem to find it hard to believe that I spent two months in the FIT dorms and didn't see the campus at all, but it's the truth. My summer wasn't about touring colleges. It was about learning the fashion industry inside and out. If I could turn back time, I'd schedule a tour and learn more about FIT and Parsons when I had the chance, but it is what it is.

Another weird thing since I've been back is Nina LeFleur, my number one rival — she's actually been *nice* to me! Well, maybe not exactly *nice*, but at least not awful like in the past. Sometimes, she'll even stop to make small talk about school and fashion. It doesn't seem like she's trying to mess with me, but it's just one more thing that makes me feel like everything changed while I was away and someone forgot to give me the new script. . . .

Xoxo — Chloe

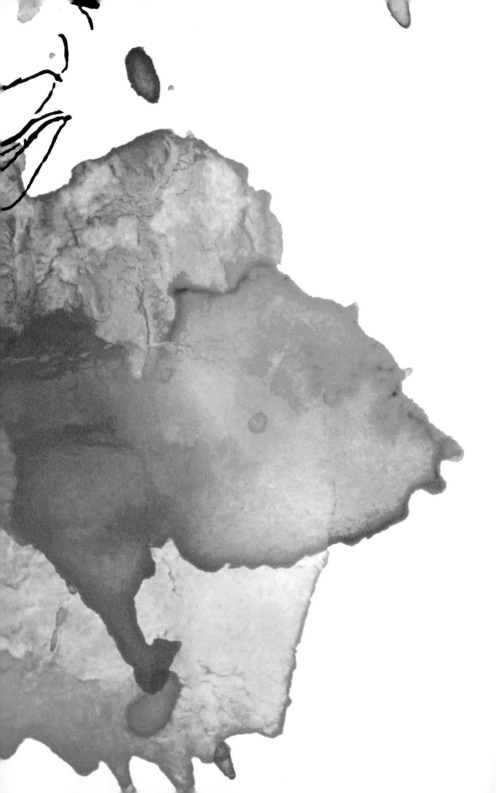

Today will be a good day, I tell myself as I hop out of bed. I've been feeling off for too long now, and it's time to get back in the swing of things. I keep telling myself that if I just *act* happy, it's bound to rub off and make me happy for real. (So far, not much luck with that.)

I start with my outfit — cute clothes are always a good pick-me-up. I'm not in the mood for bright colors today. That means I need a fun, black dress that can hold its own. I choose a sleeveless suede shift dress in black that falls just above the knee. Its embroidered square pattern keeps it from being boring, and I can add a blazer or sweater if I get chilly. Now for the shoes. My black sandals that lace up at the ankle are perfect.

"Liking the smile," my mom says when I arrive downstairs for breakfast. "I've missed it."

I give her a quick hug. "Me too. I know I've been kind of a grump lately. I just didn't realize how much I'd miss by being gone for two months. Not that I regret it. It's just that everyone seems to have all their college stuff figured out, and they've hung out all summer. I don't know exactly where I fit in."

Mom nods. "I get why you feel like that, but I know for a fact that Alex is thrilled to have you home. She's practically moved in since you got back. Which reminds me — I need to buy more of those Doritos she likes."

Alex *has* been over a lot. But most of those times, Dan's been with her. Which is fine, I guess. But when they're both here, it means double the college talk. If I'm being totally honest, Alex and Dan coming over as a couple would probably bother me less if I had Jake around. But that's not an option when he lives on the other side of the country.

"Are you going to talk to your advisor today?" Mom asks. "Maybe get some info on colleges and deadlines?"

I sigh. Clearly, college talk is unavoidable. "I don't even want to think about application deadlines."

Mom smiles. "You can't just pretend they don't exist. And we need to figure out when and how we're going to get back to New York City so you can tour both Parsons and FIT."

"I'll be fine if we can just tour FIT," I say. "It's always been my dream school. And besides, it's cheaper than Parsons."

"True, but Dad and I want you to make an informed decision. We want you to see both schools. FIDM too. That's in-state and an excellent school."

My cereal has gotten soggy, and I feel my smile slipping away. Mom is right about me trying to put off college talk, but I just wish everything could be decided already. If it could be decided without my input, that would be even better. I hate feeling so overwhelmed.

"We'll have to figure out how to pay for airfare to visit FIDM too," I mumble.

"That's right." Mom kisses the top of my hair and gently lifts my chin. "We will. Your job is to keep your mind open."

"Okay," I say. I force down my cereal and head to school. Let the Monday blues begin.

* * *

"What's with the long face?" asks Alex at my locker later that morning.

Clearly, being an actress is not in my future. I can't even pretend to be perky if I'm not feeling it. "It's Monday," I reply with a shrug. I hesitate for a moment and then add, "Plus my mom decided to start off my morning by reminding me we need to tour colleges."

Alex bites her lip, like she wants to say something, and puts her hands in the pockets of her black overalls. She has the bottoms rolled up and is wearing a cute, long-sleeved striped T-shirt underneath.

Even though I've seen Alex's new look several times already, each new outfit makes me giddy. I love that she actually *likes* going shopping now. Which is what I wish we were doing right now. Instead, I'm staring at Alex's worried face.

I sigh. "What? Spit it out."

"You really want to know?" Alex asks.

"No, but friends should be honest with each other, so speak."

"I guess I just don't think it's a bad thing that your mom brought up college tours," she says. "I looked some stuff up online, and application deadlines are in January —"

"You looked up stuff for *me*?" I interrupt.

This is so Alex. When I first heard about *Teen Design Diva* auditions — which feels like *forever* ago — I was so overwhelmed that I couldn't even look at the requirements. Alex was the one who went to the website and printed out all the information. She gave me the push and confidence I needed to apply. And don't get me wrong, I'm still super grateful. But sometimes it takes me a while to wrap my brain around something, and my best friend's pushiness can be a little . . . well . . . pushy.

Alex blushes. "Too much? I'm sorry. I was just trying to help. You've seemed a little overwhelmed since you got back from New York. I just want you to be as excited about college stuff as I am."

I take a deep breath and count slowly to ten. I know Alex means well. But this is too much for a Monday morning. Not only do I have to make appointments for college tours and figure out paying for airfare, but this conversation has reminded me how behind in the process I actually am. I only have a few months to complete my applications and turn them in.

When I don't say anything, Alex puts her hand on my arm. "Chloe, I'll help you make a schedule. Whatever you need."

I shake my head. I don't want to think about a schedule right now. What I need is to not think. Not about this anyway.

I shrug Alex's hand away. "I need to get to class," I say. "I'll talk to you about it later."

Alex's face falls, which makes me feel even worse. I know she's trying to help, but I'm not ready for that kind of help yet.

ALEX'S
OUTFIT
Design

LONG-SLEEVED
STRIPED
T-SHIRT

BLACK
OVERALLS

Style Evolution

ROLLED
CUFFS

By the time I get home from school, all I want to do is flop down on my bed and read a fashion magazine. But the conversations I had with my mom and Alex are still running around in my mind. Maybe the only way to stop their words from invading my brain is to *do* something about it.

I open my laptop and go to FIT's website first. This seems like the best place to start. It's always been my dream school, and I'm at least *somewhat* familiar with it since I stayed in the dorms there during my internship. Maybe I didn't see anything *besides* the dorms, but it's something.

I click through the different sections on the website. The campus photos look nice, and the video showing students sketching outside makes me feel at home. The different students all seem to have their own style, which

I love. It would be so boring if everyone looked the same. Some are wearing clothes that are simple and chic, like what I tend to wear. A student in a jersey dress and sneakers reminds me of Alex's sporty style. There are kids in preppier clothes too, and I admire the outfit of a girl in a pleated skirt, sleeveless white blouse, and tie. Another student is sporting a more bohemian look that makes me think of the sketches I did while people watching in NYC over the summer. The girl is wearing a crocheted top that hangs loosely over embroidered shorts, and her hair is in braids that graze the layered necklaces she's piled on.

I watch the video a little longer and then click on the *How To Apply* tab. I groan when I see I have to write an essay about why I want to attend FIT. I wish I could explain myself in clothes. It's so much easier explaining myself through my designs than through words.

With that in mind, I click on the *Portfolio Requirements* tab. The first thing on the list is another essay. My heart sinks, but I feel better when I see the topic: *Write about a hard time in a workplace.* I can handle that. My internship at Stefan Meyers definitely wasn't easy, so I'm sure I can find something to write about. The time I tried to cut corners on an assignment given to me by Laura, one of my bosses, could be a good example. Even now I shudder when I think about it. I did learn from it, though, and got another chance.

I scan the page to see what else I have to do and start to get dizzy reading through all the project descriptions. I knew I'd have to submit a portfolio of some kind, but thought it would just be a collection of my sketches. Boy, was I wrong. One part asks for samples of my designs and another wants photos of stuff I've sewn. And then there's a third task that asks applicants to create a fashion line for a pop star, imagining what he or she would wear on stage, out with friends, and lounging around.

Relax, Chloe, I tell myself, taking a deep breath. *One thing at a time. This is totally doable. You've got this.*

I print out the pages and stack the papers into a neat pile. Then I decide to take a break. That was enough for one day, right? I pick up one of my magazines and sprawl out on my bed, but I can't concentrate on the photos. A voice inside my head keeps telling me I didn't put a dent in this college thing at all. I flip through the pages of the magazine, hoping the outfits and styling tips will push the nagging voice out, but it doesn't work. I need to feel like I did *something* today.

Reluctantly, I put down my magazine and pick up an old sketchpad, flipping through until I find the sketches I drew for my *Teen Design Diva* auditions. They give me an idea, and I run to my closet. I can use some of the designs I sewed for the auditions for my FIT portfolio. The silk dress I designed for the first round of auditions was one of my favorites, but the stitching was really off, which means I can't use it. That was before I learned how to sew silk properly.

Light-bulb moment! I can email the *Design Diva* producers and ask them for photos of the designs I made while on the show. Having a concrete place to start for one part of the portfolio makes me feel better.

I look through more sketches and see one of the outfits Alex wore when she came to see me in New York during Fashion Week. I remember how excited I felt when I first saw it. The fitted black T-shirt, distressed boyfriend jeans, and studded black flats were such a surprise from her previous fashion mantra of *sweatpants chic*.

That gives me another idea — maybe one of the sections in my portfolio can be dedicated to Alex's evolving look. After all, I've definitely influenced that, and I love sketching outfits for my best friend. I start to get more excited than nervous, and scribble down some notes on my ideas. Then I draft a quick email to the *Design Diva* people asking about the photographs I'll need. Finally feeling somewhat accomplished, I close my laptop.

But what about the other colleges? the annoying voice in my head nags again. I shoo it away. So what that I don't have a pop star picked out yet? So what if I haven't looked at the requirements for Parsons and FIDM? I can probably use the same sketches for all three applications. I'm not going to think about that now. Instead, I text Jake about my afternoon accomplishments.

My phone pings almost immediately with a message back from him: *Congrats on starting the maddening process!*

I smile. Jake always gets me. It *is* a crazy process. I decide to reward my hard work with some uninterrupted magazine reading. This is what fashion should be — fun and stress-free.

BLACK T-SHIRT

ALEX'S NYC OUTFIT Sketches

FUN PRINTS

OFF-THE-SHOULDER TOP

BOYFRIEND JEANS

STUDDED FLATS

PLAID ROMPER

Day Dresses

TALL BOOTS!?!

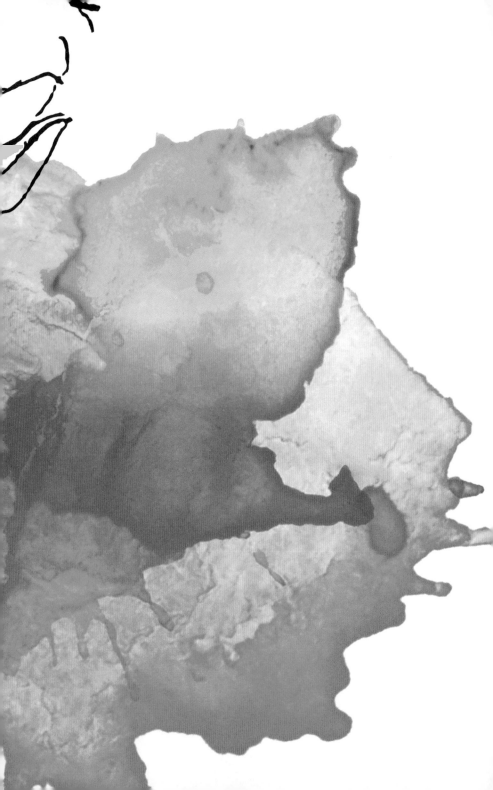

"So we're all getting a table together for this weekend's fashion show, right?" Alex asks at lunch the next day. We're sitting together with Dan, Alex's boyfriend, plus a couple of her new friends, Jada Williams and Mia Sanchez.

That morning, I told her about yesterday's successful college research. Sometimes I just need that extra nudge to get things started. To Alex's credit, she was all kinds of supportive and didn't say anything about the fact that I only looked up one college.

I didn't say anything about her new style being part of my portfolio yet. I want to surprise her and also not make her feel self-conscious about the clothes she chooses. Today she's wearing a pair of dark jeans, a lighter chambray shirt, and leopard-print flats. I make a note to sketch it when I get home.

"Is that this weekend?" I ask. I remember Alex talking about the charity fashion show when I first came back from New York, but truthfully, I'd forgotten all about it.

Alex nods. "Yeah, it's going to showcase designs for Winter Formal."

Maybe that's why I put it out of my mind. Formals involve dates. Who knows if I'll have one? Jake might have finals that week or be busy. Or just not be able to fly here. His dad lives in California, but that doesn't mean he can fly back from New York whenever he wants. I haven't mentioned Winter Formal in any of our texts. Probably because I don't want to hear his answer if it's no.

Jada laughs. "It's probably not much compared to the New York fashion scene. But apparently, it's a big deal here."

I cringe. I didn't mean to make it sound like I'm too good for the stuff here. "I didn't mean —"

"Relax," says Jada with a laugh. "I'm just kidding."

"Chloe takes things a little seriously sometimes," says Alex. "But that's why I love her." She gives me a hug. "We balance each other out."

That makes me feel better, but not understanding Jada's sense of humor is just another thing that makes me feel left out. Jada moved here over the summer from Connecticut. She seems really nice, but it was weird coming home and seeing Alex with a new friend I'd never met. She never even mentioned her when I was in New York. It's hard not to feel a little jealous when they talk about all the fun stuff they did over the summer or laugh at inside jokes I don't get. I know I'm the one who left for the summer, but sometimes it feels like Alex is the one leaving me behind.

At least Jada and I have completely different styles. I'd feel even worse if Alex had found a total Chloe replacement, but Jada has her own East Coast thing going on. Her clothes are all pretty preppy, similar to the girl I noticed in the FIT video. Preppy always makes me think serious and buttoned-up, but Jada's personality is the opposite of her style. She finds humor in just about everything. Today she's wearing an argyle sweater vest over a short-sleeved blue shirt dress. It screams Ivy League. That's good since Cornell, Princeton, and Yale are Jada's top choices. (Believe me, I've heard all about it.)

"A table would be great," I say. "Any word on the styles they're showcasing?"

"Nope," says Mia. "But I'm hoping for something a little out there and crazy."

I've hung out with Mia before, but she and Alex became really close over the summer. Mia's style is more edgy than mine. Today, she's wearing a V-neck tie-dyed sweater with bell sleeves over a distressed denim skirt. The tips of her

STUDENT DEVELOPMENT *Sketches*

CM

JADA'S PREPPY STYLE

LIGHT DENIM SHIRT

DARK DENIM JEANS

ARGYLE SWEATER VEST

ALEX'S NEW STYLE

BLUE SHIRT DRESS

TALL BLACK BOOTS

LEOPARD-PRINT FLATS

dark hair have been dyed pink. I've seen them blue and green too.

Dan takes a bite of his sandwich. "The parents are running the show, so I wouldn't hold my breath."

"Not like you'd care," says Alex. "You're lucky. You just wear a suit and call it a day. A shirt with color would be wild and crazy for you."

"That is correct," says Dan. "I'm a no-frills kind of guy."

"And that's why you're awesome," Alex says, taking his hand.

Just then my phone pings, saving me from further Alex-Dan mushiness. It's an email from one of the *Design Diva* producers with photos of all the designs I did for the show. They sent photos of everything I ever made, including my audition stuff. How sweet! I feel myself getting sentimental and pull myself together. But not fast enough.

"What's up?" Alex asks, separating herself from Dan long enough to peer at my phone.

"Just one of the producers from *Design Diva*." I show her the photos. "I emailed to get photos of the pieces I made."

"Nice! That'll help with the college application stuff, for sure."

"I can't wait until that's finished," Jada says, overhearing Alex's comment. And just like that we're off the fashion show topic and onto college talk again. "I'm applying early decision, so it's going to be crazy until the November deadline, but then I'm home free."

"Ugh!" Mia says. "I'd die if I had to submit stuff that early. But at least I don't have to make a bunch of different portfolios like Chloe. I so feel for you, girl."

"What do you mean?" I say. Clearly Mia doesn't know what she's talking about. "I'm planning to use the same designs and portfolio for all the schools."

Mia shakes her head. "My older sister is at FIDM, and she had to have different sketches for every school she applied to," she says, oblivious to Alex waving her hands in the air. Finally, Mia notices. "What are you doing? Is there a fly?"

I slump down in my chair. "No, Alex just knows all this college stuff is kind of freaking me out, and she wanted me to live in my happy place a little longer. It's just a little overwhelming."

Mia frowns. "Sorry, Chloe. I figured you already knew. My sister had all kinds of designs. I think one was amusement-park themed. I can ask her, if you want."

"No," I say weakly. "That's okay. Don't ask."

"You sure?" Mia takes out her phone, ready to make the call.

I nod and put my head in my hands. Just yesterday I was feeling terrific about my progress. Now, I see I have so much more to do. When I get home, I just want to crawl under the covers and not think about all the work ahead of me.

"So, back to the fashion show," says Dan, changing the subject, even though I know he couldn't care less about the show.

"Right," says Jada, picking up on his cue. "I'm hoping for some sleek evening dresses. Something classy."

"Chloe?" Alex says, trying to draw me in to the conversation. "How about you? What are you thinking?"

I barely hear her. All I'm thinking about are the portfolio requirements I have no interest in looking up. And an imaginary pop star whose wardrobe I need to create.

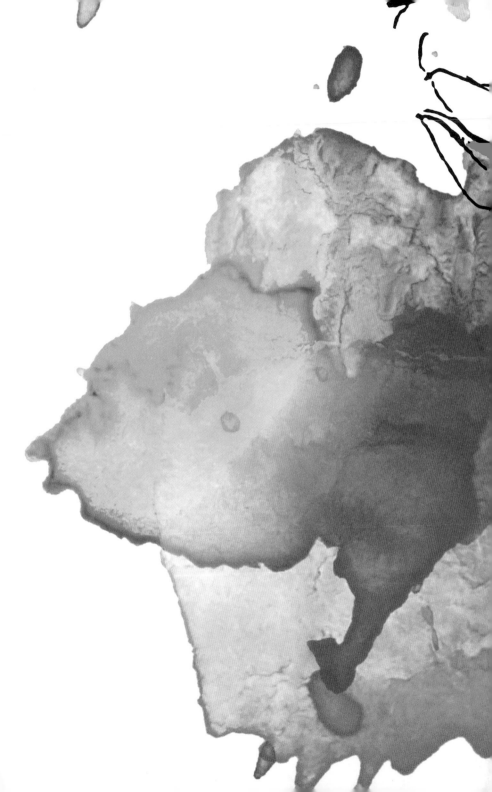

4

By Saturday, the school gym has been transformed into fashion central. You can barely tell it was ever a gym. Tables have been set up on one side, and the floor is covered in a shimmery white fabric. A stage and speakers have been placed at the front of the room, and lights surround the runway. I had my doubts about what kind of fashion show the school could pull off, but it honestly doesn't look that different from the shows in New York City.

"Wow! This is so impressive," I say to Alex when we arrive.

"I know! I didn't expect that at all," she agrees. "It reminds me of the runways in NYC from when I came to visit."

We share a smile, remembering our time together at Stefan's Fashion Week show, and I feel more in my zone than I have in weeks. I feel like Alex and I are connected, like we have our own special relationship the others don't. The fact that we're at a fashion show puts me more in my element too. For the first time in a long time, I don't feel left out.

I catch a glimpse of Nina behind the stage helping the models with some alterations and walk over. For a second, I wish I'd come back from New York sooner. Then I could be helping at the show too. But the thought quickly passes. Today, I'm glad I get to relax with my friends and not deal with the runway angst.

Alex sees some friends at a nearby table and makes her way over while I duck backstage to say hi to Nina. I'm trying to be nice because she's been civil lately. And, like it or not, Nina and I probably have the most in common when it comes to college applications.

"Hey," I say to Nina. "How's it going? Staying sane back here? Fashion shows are a lot of work."

Nina shoots me an unreadable look. "I'm sure this doesn't compare to New York, but I'm doing what I can." Her tone is a little snippy, which could be because she's stressed with last-minute details or because she thinks I've come to brag — knowing Nina, probably a little of both.

"Actually, this set-up is really amazing," I say.

Nina pauses mid-pin and glances my way. "You're not being sarcastic?"

"Nope."

Nina looks confused for a minute, but then forces a smile. "Thanks."

"Sure. Good luck."

"Where'd you disappear to?" Alex asks when I sit back down at our table.

"I just ducked backstage to say hi to Nina and see how things are going," I reply.

"Nina? You and Nina were actually having a pleasant conversation?" Alex says, looking shocked.

I shrug. "Seems like. You have to admit she's been nicer this year since I got back," I say. "Maybe she's finally decided to bury the hatchet since it's senior year."

"Hmm . . . well, I don't know. I still wouldn't trust her completely."

"We're not sharing clothes or anything just yet, but . . ." I want to say I have a feeling that Nina will understand how anxious I am about all the portfolio stuff, but I know that will make Alex feel like I'm somehow saying she *doesn't* get it.

"A fashionista doesn't change her polka dots that easily," Alex says, letting me off the hook. "That's all I'm saying."

I laugh. "Look at you trying to make a fashion analogy. That's so cute."

Alex gives me a playful shove.

"What's cute?" Jada asks just then as she and Mia arrive and grab seats at our table.

"Alex being fashion-y," I say.

Mia grins. "It does take a little getting used to," she says.

Jada looks confused. "I'm missing something, right?"

Alex blushes. "Well, let's just say that before this past summer I wasn't the put-together fashion icon you see before you." She gets out of her chair and pretends to strut down an imaginary catwalk to show off this evening's style: a black short-sleeved sweater, blue jeans with the bottom cuffs rolled up, and black chunky sandals.

We all crack up, and Alex makes her way back to her seat. Just then, the lights dim and the music starts. I immediately snap to attention.

This is where I belong.

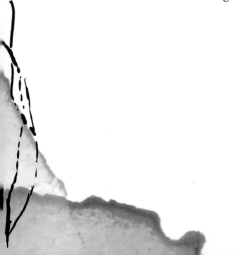

ALEX'S
OUTFIT
Design

SHORT-SLEEVED
SWEATER

Style Evolution

CHUNKY
SANDALS

ROLLED
DENIM
JEANS

Everyone focuses on the runway, and a moment later, the model walks out in a green A-line dress that falls to her knees. It has a deep V-neck, a cinched waist, and pouf sleeves. It reminds me of the party dresses Alex and I loved when we were little kids. The dress has potential, but I wouldn't wear it as is. It's a little too youthful and basic.

I take out my sketchpad and draw the design on the runway on one side, then imagine how I'd change it on the other. I make the hemline asymmetrical, so it's shorter in the front than the back. I also change the sleeves from poufy to fluted. This way, they start off fitted but then flare out by the wrists. They would look pretty in a sheer material too.

Alex leans over and peeks at my drawing. "That's beautiful," she whispers. "I would so wear that."

As the show continues, I keep one eye on the runway and the other on my sketchpad. I try to capture the dresses I love, as well as the ones I'd tweak to better fit my style.

Lola James's new song — about life in New York — floods the speakers, and I take that as a sign and doodle, *New York + fashion = Chloe's favorite things* across a new page of my sketchpad. Before I realize what I'm doing, I'm using Lola James as my model and drawing my Winter Formal designs on her.

Then it hits me — she can be my pop star for my portfolio! She's one of my favorite singers, and her songs are the perfect inspiration too. They'll give me plenty of ideas for outfits she'd wear for different occasions: out with friends, to red carpet events, or when she's just chilling on the couch writing music.

Brightly colored dresses fill the runway, and I add them to my sketchbook, changing some so that the colors act as accents rather than the majority of each dress. I change the backs too. I draw crisscross straps made of rhinestones on one sketch. On another I change the back design to a scoop back.

Remembering the art deco-inspired work I did for Laura and Taylor during my internship, I spice up some designs with embellishments. One dress gets a beaded bodice, while another gets a V-neck studded with crystals.

By the time the fashion show draws to a close an hour later, I have more than ten pages of sketches, my pop star picked out, and a new attitude.

* * *

"That was really fun," says Jada after the models do their final walk on the runway. "It must have taken a lot of work to put it all together."

"You have no idea," says a voice behind me.

I turn around and see Nina standing there. "You should be proud," I tell her.

"I am, but those designs . . ." she trails off and frowns.

"They were kind of lame, right?" says Mia. "No offense."

"None taken," says Nina. "The parents in charge had a very specific vision of what they wanted. They didn't really care when I tried to say we wouldn't wear most of those styles."

Alex clears her throat. "Chloe did some really amazing sketches during the show."

"Yeah?" says Jada. "Can we see?"

I shyly open my sketchbook and show them my designs. "They're just doodles," I mumble. "The full sketch will look better."

SCHOOL FASHION SHOW *Designs*

Original Look

POUF SLEEVES

FLUTED SLEEVES

HIGH-LOW SKIRT

A-LINE DRESS

New Look!

"Stop," says Mia. "These are fantastic. I'd wear any of those."

"Same here," says Jada.

Nina pushes her way in beside Mia to get a better look. "They *are* good," she says grudgingly. "Not exactly *my* style but nice."

Alex snorts and gives me an I-told-you-so look. "What exactly is *your* style?" she asks.

"Something a little more feminine and refined," says Nina. That vision matches with the long-sleeved floral romper she's wearing.

"You know," says Jada, "I have a great idea. What if Chloe and Nina designed our Winter Formal dresses?"

"That would be awesome!" Mia agrees. "I bet lots of girls would be into that."

"Together?" Nina says, shooting me a slightly panicked look. "I don't —"

I'm all for designing dresses . . . but not with Nina. It's one thing that we're not mortal enemies anymore. But it's another to work together, especially when we have such different design styles.

"Yeah," I chime in. "I don't think that would work. Nina said her vision is different from mine and —"

"Relax, you two," Jada interrupts. "I bet there are girls whose tastes lean more toward Nina's and others who'd prefer Chloe's vision. Besides, it will be a lot of work. No way can one of you handle it all."

"I can handle a lot," Nina mutters.

I shoot her a look. "Me too," I say. After all, I've designed stuff that went down the runway during Fashion Week. I can definitely handle a few dresses for a Santa Cruz dance.

"Okay, then," says Alex. "It's decided. Let's start spreading the word."

A week later, my room looks like a tornado went through it. My floor is covered with sketches, fabric samples, and containers filled with embellishments. Since Nina and I agreed to design dresses for Winter Formal, I've had appointments almost every day. My parents have been really supportive, but when two girls showed up during dinner a few days ago, they drew the line. From now on, I'm not allowed to have more than one appointment per day. On weekends, I can have more as long as they don't interfere with dinner or family plans.

I enlisted Alex's help in making a schedule, and she was thrilled. She loves organization and was so excited to keep track of the materials used and scheduling appointments. She even offered to keep track of any input Mimi — my favorite local boutique owner — provided. Nina and I realized that we didn't have time to design the dresses *and* make them, so Mimi graciously offered to help with the sewing.

"This will look amazing on my college applications!" Alex exclaimed when I asked. "What school wouldn't want a future business major who's already doing business stuff in high school?"

That got me thinking — not only can I make my Winter Formal designs part of my portfolio, this could also be the start of my own label. Don't get me wrong — I know that's a *big* jump. I mean, I'm confident in my designing, but starting my own label is a lot of pressure. But it's what I want more than anything else. So I'm trying to be positive and not typical Chloe who doubts herself at too many turns.

"Who's next on our list?" I ask Alex when she shows up for our Saturday afternoon appointment.

Alex pulls out her laptop and pulls up a spreadsheet she made. "Sophia Gonzalez. Do you know her?"

"I've seen her around. She's in the animal rights club, and she played Glinda the Good Witch in *The Wizard of Oz* last year. I think she has pretty girly, feminine style."

Alex makes a face when I say the word *girly*, as if there's nothing worse than that.

I roll my eyes. "Girly can be really pretty. I can work with that."

Just then, my mom knocks on my bedroom door. "Your next client is here," she says very seriously. She can be really silly sometimes, but I do like the sound of that. It's like I'm running a real business.

"Hi, Chloe!" Sophia says, walking into my room. She's wearing floral pants and a lacy, off-the-shoulder blouse. Her hair is swept up with a lace ribbon. "Thanks for squeezing me in. I'm so excited about this! It's going to be so cool to have a custom dress! I even brought some designs."

"Very cool," I say, taking the papers from her hand. "It's really helpful if I have a clear idea of what you want."

"I actually showed these to Nina first," Sophia says, "but she said you might be a better fit."

"I'll bet she did," Alex mutters under her breath.

I shoot Alex a look that says *zip it* and then turn back to Sophia. "I'm sure I can come up with something based on these. Why don't you have a seat while I look through them, okay?"

The fact that Nina sent Sophia here gives me a bad feeling, but I try to shrug it off and look at the papers — photos from magazines pasted together with some of Sophia's ideas drawn in — with an open mind. I do this kind of thing when brainstorming too, but as I flip through Sophia's ideas, I realize there's a major difference. The designs I pick go together. These don't — at all.

SOPHIA'S INSPIRATION *Sketches*

CINDERELLA-TYPE BALL GOWN

TULLE

SEQUINS

FULL SKIRT

OFF-THE-SHOULDER

BIG BOW

DROP WAIST

One page shows a Cinderella-type ball gown bottom paired with a sequined top, and Sophia had added poufy sleeves similar to what we saw at the fashion show last week. Another combination is a skirt with layers of tulle and an off-the-shoulder velvet top. I see more and more mismatched combinations as I flip through the stack. I like an element of each design, but the way Sophia seems to envision them together is a little bizarre.

I feel Sophia's eyes on me and force myself to smile. There's more to being a fashion designer than just drawing. I have to learn to sell my ideas to clients too, or there's no way I'll make it as a designer. I take a deep breath. Here goes nothing.

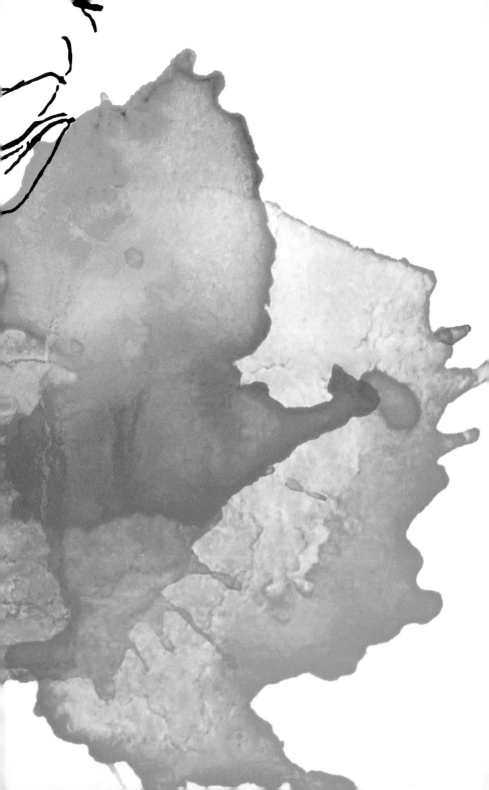

7

"You have a lot of great ideas," I start, hoping I'm being tactful. I rack my brain, trying to figure out how to phrase the next part so it doesn't hurt her feelings. I know how crushing it can be to present an idea you think is terrific, only to be told it won't work at all — I had plenty of experience with that during *Design Diva* and my internship. I tap my pencil on my lip. "A lot of great ideas," I repeat to give myself more time to think.

I remember how helpful it was when the *Design Diva* judges or my internship supervisors told me how to fix my designs but also emphasized what was good about them. The positive stuff gave me confidence and made me feel less hopeless about the things I had to fix.

Alex snorts beside me, and I give her a stern look. She pretends to study her spreadsheet.

Sophia looks at me expectantly. "So, the thing is," I begin, "I'm not sure how some of these designs fit together." Sophia's face falls, and I rush to say something promising. "But, I think it's just a matter of moving some things around. There's definitely stuff here I can use."

Sophia perks up. "Great! I mean, it doesn't have to look *exactly* like it does in my pictures. I'm open to input. Kind of."

I look at the designs again. "Maybe the best place to start is by you telling me which styles are your absolute favorites. Then, we'll go from there."

I hand Sophia her designs, and Alex gives me a thumbs-up as Sophia scans her drawings.

About ten minutes later, Sophia has circled a few styles on each page. "I really like a fairy-tale princess type of look," says Sophia, blushing. "Something you'd see in Disney movies. Is that too silly?"

This sparks something for me. I have the perfect Disney princess in mind, and it's a perfect fit for Winter Formal. "Not silly at all! Actually, you gave me an idea. One sec."

I draw a very rough sketch of a strapless ice-blue gown. I also add a belt in a slightly darker shade of blue to create some contrast and define the waist. When I'm done sketching, I show my picture to Sophia, and she gasps.

"Is that a good gasp?" I ask.

SWEETHEART
NECKLINE

SOPHIA'S
DRESS IDEA
Sketches

SKINNY
STRAPS & SCOOP
NECK

- *Icy*
- *Sweet*
- *Sheer*

BEADED
NECKLINE

LACE-COVERED
BODICE

SHEER
SLEEVES

"Definitely!" says Sophia. "I love this skirt. It looks like a ball gown."

"Yay! That's what I was going for. Now for the top. What kind of neckline would you like? You can do a sweetheart. That would look pretty." I make a slight alteration to the sketch to show her what I mean.

"It would," says Sophia, "but I'm not totally sold on strapless to be honest. I don't want to be pulling my dress up all night. And is there any way to add lace?"

I stifle a sigh. After all, the client is always right — at least that's what they say. Instead, I focus on my sketch and add straps and a scoop neck, covering the bodice of the dress with lace.

"Wait," says Sophia. "Maybe not lace. Beading?"

This time I can't help it — a small sigh sneaks out. But I turn back to the page and add beading along the neckline. I use a colored pencil to add shades of gold and silver. It looks like a covering of snowflakes.

"Oh, that's pretty!" Sophia says, peering at the sketch. "But wait — maybe beading isn't right. Maybe sequins?"

I take a deep breath, and Alex types hard on her laptop.

"Um, Alex, would you mind getting me a glass of water, please?" I'm afraid if she stays here longer she'll snipe at Sophia for being so indecisive.

"Gladly," says Alex, looking relieved.

"Sorry," Sophia says to me when Alex is gone. "It's like I see it in my head but can't exactly explain it. Has that ever happened to you?"

"All the time," I say. I think for a few minutes, trying to mentally piece together all the different elements Sophia has mentioned. "Okay, I think you'll like this."

I flip to a clean page in my sketchbook, and get to work. I keep the basic silhouette of the dress the same but add sleeves and a higher neckline, making them both sheer — I'll have Mimi use illusion netting for that. I keep the fuller skirt, but change it to tulle. Then I add tons of crystal and floral appliques to the top and midsection, thinning them out near the bottom, turning the dress into a shimmery winter wonderland of a design.

When I'm done, I show Sophia the sketch. Her eyes light up. "This is exactly what I was thinking. No, it's much better than what I was thinking. Thank you!"

I smile, relieved that I finally nailed it and have a happy client. "I'll make a copy of this for Mimi. Here's her number. Call her to arrange a fitting for your measurements."

"Thank you so much, Chloe," Sophia says as Alex walks back in. "I'll be sure to thank Nina for sending me to you."

"Don't worry," I say, smiling. I can't wait to see the look on Nina's face when I tell her how fun it was designing Sophia's dress. "I'll be sure to tell her myself."

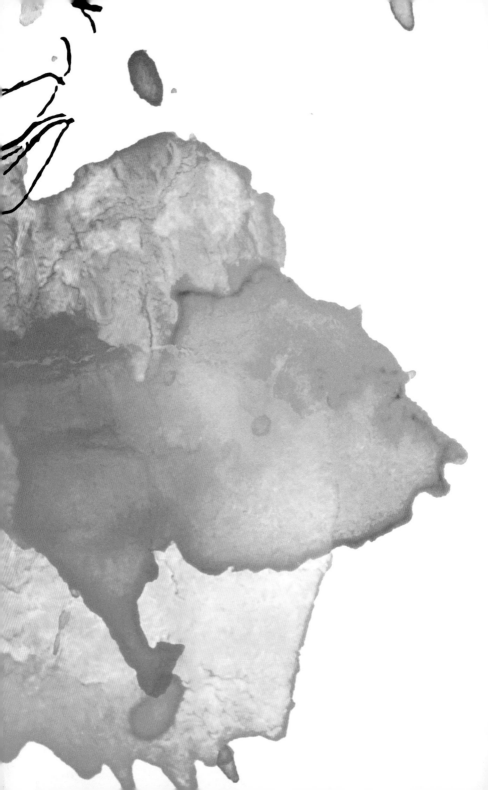

8

The next day, as promised, I head over to Mimi's Thrifty Threads to drop off the sketch for Sophia's dress. Mimi's store has the power to make everything better. It always has. It was my refuge even before my *Design Diva* days. There's just something about it that feels warm and welcoming.

I wave to Mimi as I walk in and busy myself by looking at the clothing on the racks while she helps the last customer of the day. Right away I spot several new designs, like a silk blouse with a suede collar. There's another blouse with the materials in reverse — suede shirt and silk collar. After working on collars during my internship, I notice them a lot more than I used to.

I've always admired the risks Mimi takes in her designs. She's never been afraid to experiment with colors or patterns. She says it's from her time working as a designer and seamstress in New York City. It made her open to a range of styles and people's tastes. Today, for example, she's wearing a bright orange blouse, black leggings with thigh-high boots, and a large belt with a gold clasp in the middle. She has her hair pulled back with an orange and gold scarf.

I'm lost in thought, thinking about my internship, my portfolio, and the Winter Formal designs when Mimi walks over. "What did you bring me today?" she asks.

"Another design for Winter Formal," I say, handing over the copy of the sketch I made.

"It's very pretty," says Mimi, looking it over. "What kind of fabric were you thinking?"

"Probably tulle for the skirt, illusion netting to cover the bodice and sleeves, and then lots of beading. I really want the illusion netting to act as a base for the embellishments more than anything else."

"Got it," Mimi says, making a few notes on the sketch. "So now that that's done, what else is on your mind?"

I laugh. "How do you know something is on my mind?"

Mimi gives me a knowing look. "Darling, don't be offended, but you're not that hard to read. Especially when I know you so well."

I laugh. "I guess it saves me the trouble of figuring out how to bring stuff up."

Mimi goes behind the counter and plugs in her brewing machine. Then, she pours each of us a cup of tea. Mimi's mug is shaped like a handbag, and mine is shaped like a high-heeled shoe.

"Mmm," I say. "Smells like vanilla." I take a sip of the warm, comforting beverage. Mimi doesn't push me to talk, which I appreciate. I take another swallow of tea. "The thing is," I finally say, "I'm kind of freaking about the whole college application thing, but I'm not exactly sure why. I just can't seem to stop procrastinating and get focused. So far I've only looked at the portfolio requirements for FIT."

"How were those?" Mimi asks.

"Doable. I can use some of the designs I already have. And I'm planning to use Alex's evolving style as another theme. They also want a wardrobe for a pop star, and I chose Lola James," I say.

"Well, it seems like you have that application under control then."

"I guess," I say with a shrug, "but that's just one school. I'm planning to apply to Parsons and FIDM too. Oh, I almost forgot — there's an essay component too, which I hate."

Mimi waves her hand like she's swatting away my last statement. "The essay is no big deal. That's one thing that should be similar from school to school."

I put my chin in my hands. Mimi's words should be reassuring, but they're not. "What if the requirements for the other schools are too much? What if I won't have time to do them?"

"You won't have time if you keep worrying about them instead of starting," Mimi says. "You're a capable young woman, Chloe, but you have a bad habit of psyching yourself out time and time again. The important thing is that you get going on your other portfolios. Just rip off the Band-Aid, and get to it."

I look down at my mug, studying it silently. I want to say it's not possible — that I have too much going on and she wouldn't understand — but this conversation is feeling familiar. I was in the same mindset before the *Design Diva* competition. I was so worried I wouldn't be able to put anything together that I almost didn't audition at all. Then too, Mimi's tough love made me see I needed to stop worrying and just start.

I'm still not ready, though, so I stall. "Then, there's the whole airfare thing. How can I afford to visit both New York City and LA? I feel bad asking my parents to pay for plane tickets, especially since I was just in NYC all summer."

"Have you not been keeping up with the new season of *Design Diva?*" Mimi asks.

I shrug. "Sort of. They're just taping now. It hasn't aired yet."

Mimi sighs. "Yes, and where is it taping?"

Suddenly I understand what she's getting at. Why didn't I think of this before? "LA! Oh, I should email the producers or the judges and see if they're planning to have me be a guest judge like last season. If they say yes, maybe I can combine that with a tour of FIDM while I'm there. I bet the show would fly me to LA."

Mimi claps her hands. "There you go! Good job being proactive."

"But what if they say no?"

"Then they say no, and we think of a plan B. Stop thinking of things that can go wrong," Mimi says firmly. "You're not doing yourself any favors by thinking like that."

I finish my tea. I feel better and ready — or at least *readier* — to dive into the portfolio requirements for Parsons and FIDM. "Thanks, Mimi."

Mimi smiles at me. "You got it, kiddo. Remember, I'm always here for you. And a word of warning — don't be overwhelmed when you see everything you need to do. It's been a while since I applied, but I remember the requirements being fairly extensive. Just take a deep breath and start at the beginning. You can do it."

"Right. Band-Aid off and plunging in." I give Mimi a hug and then rush out of her store, heading home before this new take-charge attitude wears off.

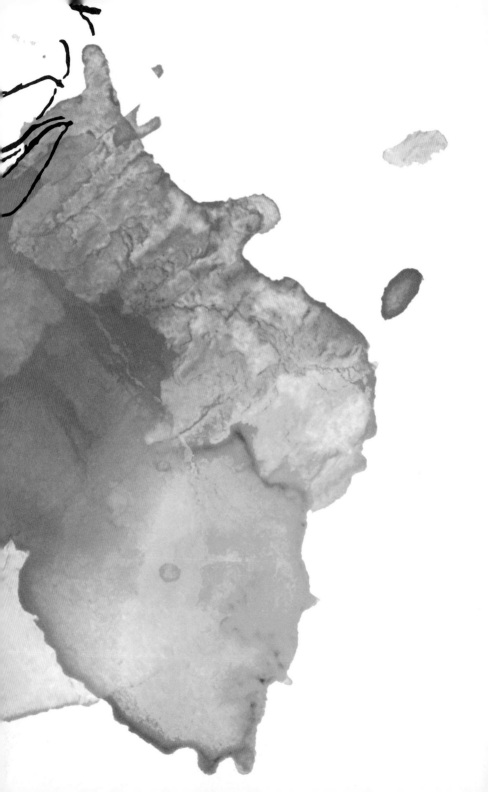

"Mimi needs to start charging for her advice," my mom says when I run into the kitchen, full of new energy, and explain where I've been.

"We'd go broke," I say with a laugh. "Speaking of, she helped me come up with a great idea for the FIDM tour. I'm going to email the producers and judges and ask if there are any plans for me to come be a guest judge on the show this season. They're taping in LA, and —"

"FIDM is in LA," my mom finishes.

"Right."

"That would be a big help, Chloe. A really big help."

The look of relief on Mom's face makes me feel guilty. I've spent so much time obsessing over being overwhelmed that I haven't given much thought to how much college visits and applications — not to mention tuition — are going to cost my parents.

I give my mom a big hug and head to my room. I open my laptop and quickly type up an email to ask about the possibility of guest judging in LA. I re-read it a few times to make sure I'm not sounding too pushy. I don't want them to think I'm asking for a free ticket — but I'm hoping it'll work out. Fingers crossed.

Next, I take a deep breath and go to the portfolio requirements on FIDM's website. One of the tasks — to showcase five or six designs that highlight a personal style — is similar to FIT. It doesn't say it has to be *my* personal style. This means I can use the sketches I'm doing to capture Alex's evolving style.

The other requirement is different: *Pick a season, and create a fashion line for that time of year. You must create six to eight designs, ranging from everyday looks to eveningwear, that showcase your theme. Be creative.*

I read the instructions three times, trying to understand what they want. It kind of makes sense, but what season? The *everyday looks to eveningwear* line sparks something in my memory. The outfit I designed for the *Teen Design Diva* finale — the dress that won me my internship — could be worn in the daytime and in the evening. It had a removable collar and peplum. Maybe that wouldn't quite work here, but I could play around with convertible tops or change a look by adding small details, like accessories or a dressy skirt.

I open to a clean page in my sketchpad and write *FIDM* at the top, but then pause. What season should I tackle? I'm a California girl at heart, so summer makes the most sense. I doodle shorts and halter-tops on the edges of my paper as I think. Then, I play with the halter-top design by changing the thickness of the straps. I change the sketch more by adding a collar and making the top tighter and then blousy.

Hmm . . . halters can easily be played down or up. I look at my drawings and have a light-bulb moment — bathing suits! Those scream *summer* and there are so many possibilities. I could do fancy halter-tops, mismatched separates, or a cute, retro one-piece.

I do a few quick sketches so I don't forget my ideas and then plunge into the Parsons site while I'm on a roll. I'm all in now and don't want to give myself a chance to back out again.

The portfolio requirements seem pretty similar at first glance. Another essay: *Where do you see yourself after college?* That's actually kind of easy. I see myself with my own Chloe Montgomery label — a big *C* and *M* intertwined within a circle. As a parting gift when my internship ended, Stefan replaced his initials with mine on the back pocket of

FIDM INSPIRATION Sketches

Halter Tops & Shorts

BOW NECK TIE

RUFFLES

PEPLUM

PATTERN

COLLARS

SKORT

POLKA DOTS

SCALLOPED EDGE

CM logo on back pocket!!

a pair of jeans. It was the best gift ever and made me feel like having my initials on my own designs would be truly possible one day.

Okay, one last piece to look at. Parsons's main portfolio task is to create a line of clothing with one theme in mind. Wow! I couldn't have dreamed for a better project. This is exactly what I'm doing with the Winter Formal dresses I'm designing. They even have two themes — formalwear and winter-inspired!

I'm feeling so on top of things I can't resist sharing. I text Jake: *Got the requirements for all three schools down. I'm all in now!*

Jake texts back almost immediately. *There's no messing with you! New York better watch out.*

I smile and type, *New York, huh? Not LA?*

This time it takes a few seconds for his message to come through. He sends a picture of a smiley face that's blushing, along with this text: *Well . . . yeah. LA too. But you know what I'm hoping for . . . miss you and hope to see you soon!*

I blush and reply that I miss him too, all the while hoping the *see you soon* part of his text is sooner rather than later.

10

"You did all this yesterday?" Alex looks impressed the next afternoon when she arrives at my house, and I show her my sketchpad, as well as printouts of the portfolio requirements for Parsons and FIT.

"Yep. Jumping in. I emailed the *Design Diva* judges and producers too. I'm hoping I can combine a guest-judging opportunity with a visit to FIDM. Mimi gave me the idea."

"That's really great," says Alex. "I'm proud of you. Kick-butt Chloe, taking charge!"

"Thanks," I say. "Now, back to work. Who's our appointment today?"

Alex glances at her watch and pulls up her spreadsheet. "Tess Peltzer is next on our list. She should be here any minute."

I groan. "She's kind of high maintenance. I mean, the stuff she wears to school is what I'd wear to, I don't know, a red carpet event? Can you imagine what she's going to want for a formal dress?"

"Girls, Tess is here," my mom says just then, peeking into my room.

"Hey, ladies," Tess says, pushing open my bedroom door. She's wearing a row of bangle bracelets that go midway up her arm, lace-up metallic gold sandals, black silk shorts, and a cream top.

Alex raises her eyebrows. She and I are both in frayed denim shorts.

"Hi, Tess," I say. "Have a —"

"Here's what I'm thinking," Tess interrupts before I can even invite her to sit down. "Valentino meets flea market."

I stare at her. Those two things are about as opposite as they get. I open my mouth to tell her that's not exactly feasible, but something tells me she won't want to hear that.

"Let's see your vision," I say instead. I was able to think of something for Sophia. I can do it again.

Tess thrusts a page from a magazine into my hands. "Something like this?" she says.

I study the image. The dress pictured *is* beautiful, but its elaborate embroidery and feathered skirt would fit in better at the Oscars than at Winter Formal. There's no way Mimi will have time to sew something like this. I study the picture to try and figure out how to tone it down so it looks like something someone in high school would wear.

"I brought this photo too," Tess says, handing me another magazine page. "It's different than what I usually wear, but it looks fun."

"Oooh!" I say. "I can definitely work with this one. I love the color." Tess's new design is more doable. The lace gives it a romantic feel, and it's more budget friendly.

Tess looks longingly at the first picture she gave me. "I think you're right," she finally says. "The second one probably makes more sense. I've been saving up my babysitting money, but it's not enough for the feathered gown."

"Sorry," I say.

"It's fine. I know a lot of people are doing winter-themed dresses, but I want to stand out. I want something bold. Maybe red."

"Red," I repeat. "That will definitely stand out."

Tess looks pleased. "Definitely. Think of it as fire and ice. Most of the other girls will be ice, but I'll be unique as fire."

"Unique it is," I say. The goal is for the customer to be happy. And it will look pretty amazing in my portfolio. I imagine a sea of dresses in shades of blue, with the red in the middle. Scrawled across the top will be the words *Fire and Ice*. *Fire* will be in red and will look like it's ablaze, and *Ice* will be in cool blue with icicles hanging from the letters. What a great name for a fashion line!

TESS'S
FINAL DRESS
Design

FIRE
RED

Elegance with
a "pop"

MERMAID
SHAPE

LACE
DETAILS

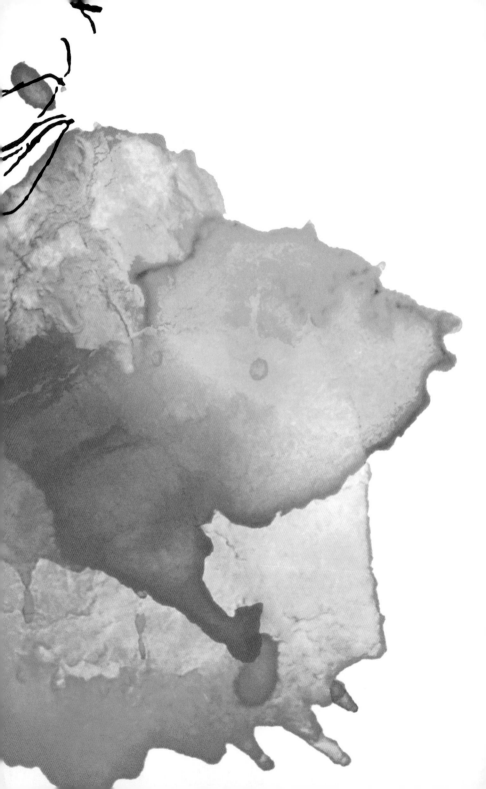

11

The next day at school, I'm floating on cloud nine. I'm sitting at lunch, and Mia, Jada, and Alex are all talking about how excited everyone is about my dress designs. I'm wearing a pink eyelet dress, which matches my happy, slightly blushing face.

"Don't be embarrassed, Chloe," says Mia, noticing my pink cheeks. "Enjoy the praise."

"I am enjoying it," I say. "But I'll never get used to being the center of attention."

"We'll stop complimenting you," Alex teases.

"Nah, I can handle it. Keep going," I say, making everyone laugh. Just then, my phone pings. It's an email from Jasmine, one of the *Design Diva* judges. My heart beats quickly as I open it.

Dear Chloe,

I just talked to the producers about your email and wanted to reach out. I'm so glad you wrote! Someone from the show was going to contact you, but you beat us to it. We'd love to have you come and be a guest judge. The producers are still finalizing details, but I think they're looking at Monday, a week from today. I know that's short notice, but they'll book a flight to LA, car to and from the airport, and hotel for both you and your mom as soon as you confirm.

You mentioned FIDM in your email as well. I still have a contact there and can put you in touch if you'd like to schedule a tour.

See you soon!
Jasmine

"Alex!" I say. "Check this out." I show her the email.

"That's awesome!" says Alex. "And how cool of her to put you in touch with someone at FIDM. But whatever will you stress about now?" She gives me a wink.

"Haha," I say, but Alex is right. Sometimes it seems I'm not totally comfortable unless there's something to worry about. Maybe it's just that I need to look at a problem from all angles so I can be prepared for potential issues. Let's go with that. Over-preparedness is good, right?

"You'll need so many outfits," says Mia. She counts off on her fingers. "One for exploring LA, another for the college tour, another for judging, another . . ." Her voice trails off as she ticks off ten other outfits.

"Mia, I'll probably only be there for a few days."

"You have to be ready for anything," Mia says. I'm glad I'm not the only one who over-prepares.

"Of course," Alex agrees with faux seriousness. "You never know who you'll run into. It's LA, after all."

"That means another outfit!" says Mia. "Something for going out in LA."

"I'll be there with my mom," I remind her. "I don't think we'll be doing much going out in LA." But even as I say it, I can't help but picture an outfit that would look good among the who's who crowd of LA. Maybe something edgy, different from my usual style. I draw it on my sketchpad. Black-and-white checkered pants, gray V-neck blouse, black suede jacket, and black ankle boots.

"I love that!" Mia squeals. "I'm going to LA just so I can wear that."

"Remember everything," says Alex. "That way when I visit you there next year, I'll know what to expect."

That evening, I take out my sketchpad and draw more of Alex's style for my portfolio. She's been on my brain since lunchtime. Today, she wore a black leather jacket over a white T-shirt dress and black open-toed sandals that clasped above the ankle. This time last year, those sandals would have been high-tops and the dress a baggy pair of jeans. I draw the old look beside the new one to show contrast.

I'm sketching Alex for my portfolio, but it's also a way to help me think through what she said at lunch. I know she's hoping I choose FIDM because it will be close to the California colleges she's applying to. And I'd love to be close to her too. Not hanging out with her all summer

ALEX'S STYLE *Designs*

New Look

BLACK LEATHER JACKET

T-SHIRT

BAGGY JEANS

T-SHIRT DRESS

HIGH-TOP SNEAKERS

OPEN-TOED SANDALS

Old Look

was hard, and I'm not looking forward to spending a year without her. Going to FIDM would also mean I would be closer to my parents. Being without them all summer wasn't easy. At least when I was filming *Design Diva*, my mom got to stay with me in New York City, but after I won and started my internship, I was flying solo.

There are a lot of things pulling me toward FIDM, I realize, but there's just something about New York City. Jake's there, of course, but it's so much more than that. Until I lived there, I never thought I'd be into the noise and crowds. I was surprised that I not only blended in, but that by the end of the internship, it felt like a second home. When I first came back to Santa Cruz, the silence was weird. For the first week, I had to play a noise app to fall asleep. It's weird that I can miss a place I only knew for a few short months.

I start to make a list of pros and cons but don't get very far. I realize I won't be able to make a true, accurate list until I've visited all the schools. FIT has always been my dream school, but that's because I didn't know that much about Parsons or FIDM. It was one of those things I decided as a kid and just went with. I'd always loved designing and had heard about all these designers who went there — people like Calvin Klein and Michael Kors. I wanted to be just like them.

But I'm seventeen now. I can't make a choice that will affect my whole life based on something I decided as a kid. But I can't help but think it would be so much easier if I could.

* * *

At dinner, I feel my parents' eyes on me. I told them the good news about Jasmine's email when I got home from school, so I know they're surprised to see me being quiet.

"What's up, kid?" asks my dad. "You got such good news today. Why the long face?"

"What if I love FIDM?" I blurt out.

My mom and dad exchange confused looks. "And that would be bad because . . . ?" my mom says.

"Because it means I'd have to choose between California and New York."

"I see," my dad says slowly. "And that isn't something you thought about before?"

"I don't know," I mutter. "Kind of. Way back in my mind. But this trip makes it more real. I don't know if I can picture myself at FIDM."

"That might change once we see the campus and learn more about the school," says my mom.

"Then if it does, I'll have to pick."

My dad chuckles. "Honey, you're going to have to decide either way. Although, you could always hope they reject you. Problem solved."

My mom and I laugh. "Okay, okay. I'm worrying too much again," I say.

"You are," my mom agrees, "and I'm here to tell you that everything will be fine. No matter what happens."

"That's right," my dad agrees. "And while I won't lie and say we wouldn't love having you closer to home, you have an amazing opportunity ahead of you. We want you to choose what's best for *you*. Experience has shown us that you can handle anything thrown at you. That won't change whether you're at FIDM, FIT, or Parsons. Take everything one step at a time."

"Exactly," Mom adds. "Keep an open mind. Just think of all the great things coming up."

I give my parents a grateful smile. Their support means so much, and I know I'm lucky to have them. They're right about the opportunities I've been given. I need to focus on how it can all go right. I imagine myself on the set of *Teen Design Diva*, walking through LA, and wearing my perfect college tour outfit. There *are* great things ahead. And if I let myself experience them without any strings, there will be many more.

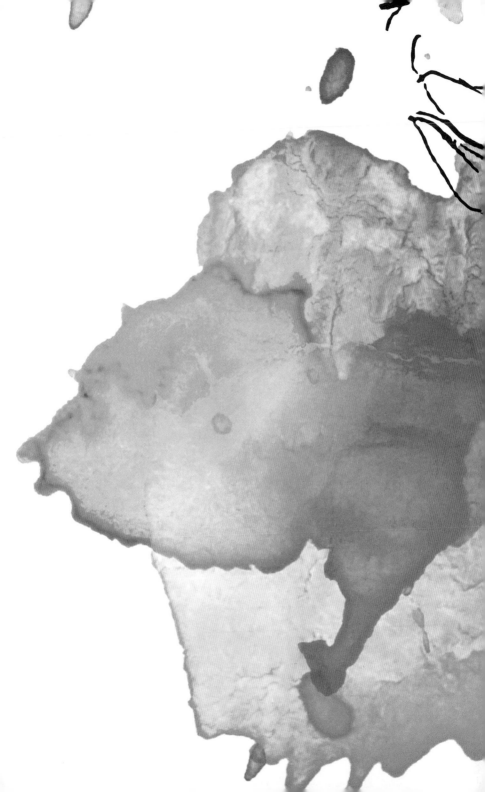

Dear Diary,

It took almost a month of being back home, but I think things are finally starting to come together on the college application front. I felt so behind when I first got back from New York — in school and in life. (Especially since Alex managed to make a bunch of new friends *and* get a new boyfriend while I was gone.) I spent a few weeks just blocking out the application process. Thankfully, Mimi helped me realize I needed to stop psyching myself out. I have to start researching and planning, or I'll never finish applications by January's deadlines.

Soooo . . . I looked up the requirements for my top choice schools — FIT, FIDM, and Parsons — and started putting together my portfolio for each one. I also have a school visit to FIDM right around the corner. I'm really lucky to be tying my visit in with guest judging for the current season of *Teen Design Diva*. Not only do I get to be a part of the show again, but the production team is paying for my flight and hotel, which is a huge help. (Touring schools that are all a plane ride away definitely adds up!)

Honestly, though, I don't know where I'll end up. On the one hand, New York has always been my dream — I loved it there this summer, and Jake is there.

But on the other hand, my friends and family are all in California . . .

Oh! I almost forgot to mention what else has been going on since my brain entered college mode. My school's Winter Formal is in December, and Nina and I are designing some of the girls' dresses! The good news is that I can use the designs I'm creating in my college portfolios. The bad news is that they're *a lot* of work; everyone has a different idea of what they want, and it's up to me to make each vision into something wearable.

I'm so excited to be designing again, and it's fun to imagine these dresses as the start of my own label — way in the future, I know! — but I'm hoping I didn't take on too much . . .

Well, the car is here to take Mom and me to the airport for the LA trip. Wish me luck!

Xoxo — Chloe

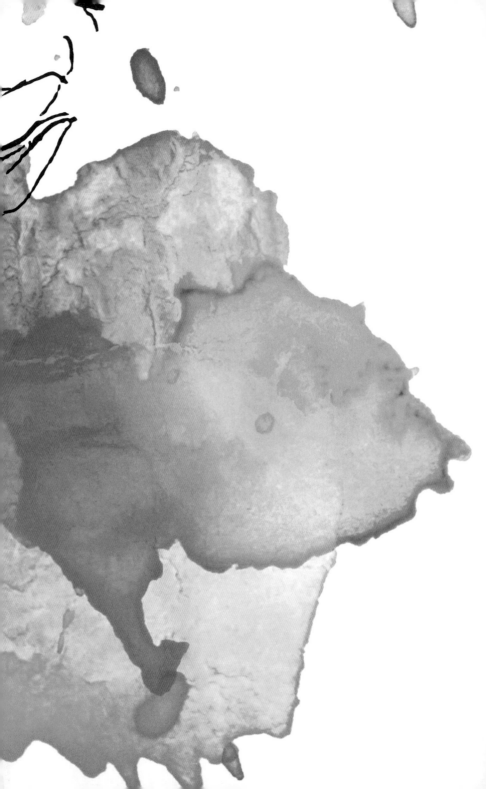

When my mom and I land in LA, the airport is a madhouse. But after my time in New York City, the noise and crowds don't bother me. In fact, the hustle and bustle is sort of comforting. I've missed this.

Mom shakes her head and smiles at me. "You look like you're actually enjoying the pushing and shoving." She grabs onto my sleeve as someone bumps into her.

"I better be careful, or I'll like it here," I say. I mean it as a joke, but it's the truth too. Part of me wants to like LA and FIDM, but there's another part of me that doesn't. Not liking it would make it easier because then I wouldn't have to choose between here and the schools in New York.

"Speaking of," Mom continues as she navigates us toward baggage claim, "please remind me what time our FIDM tour is."

I see a mom holding the hand of a toddler, which is obviously so the little boy doesn't get lost. As my mom grips my arm tighter, I smile. She's holding on to me so *she* doesn't get lost. The noise and crowds may make me excited, but they seem to make my mom nervous.

"Two o'clock," I say. "That's in three hours, which gives us time to get to our hotel, change clothes, and grab lunch."

The changing clothes part is key. I don't want to go on the college tour in my current outfit. The long-sleeved striped T-shirt, ripped jeans, and yellow sandals I'm wearing are fine for a plane ride and hanging out in an airport, but I'd like something a little more stylish for touring a fashion college.

My mom absently bites her nails, and I give her a hug. "Thanks for coming with me. I know this isn't exactly your scene," I say.

Mom gives me a smile and loosens her grip on my arm. "I'd better get used to it. Whether it's here or in New York, this is clearly your thang."

I burst out laughing at her choice of words. "My *what?*"

Mom blushes. "Isn't that what you kids say?"

"Not really," I say, still giggling as I grab our suitcases off the carousel. My mom has always been so supportive of everything I've done. I'm really going to miss her, no matter which college I go to.

I must be staring at her because Mom says, "What? Are you trying to get over how uncool I am?"

I smile at her. "No, nothing like that. I'm just thinking about how lucky I am to have you."

* * *

"Now this is more my speed," Mom says as we relax at a table in the outdoor seating area of a café near FIDM. Even though it's in the middle of the city, it somehow doesn't attract city noise. Or maybe it's just an illusion created by the restaurant's soft décor and the oversized umbrellas shading each table and shielding us from the other patrons as well as city traffic.

"I read about this place in a magazine," I say, grabbing a breadstick out of a breadbasket lined with pink paper. "Celebrities like to come here because of the privacy."

"Perfect for you, then," Mom says with a wink. "You need to keep the paparazzi at bay."

I laugh. "Please. I think my fifteen minutes are up." Although since we have our interview after this, I *am* dressed to impress in a white, open-weave sweater, faux-leather shorts, and black flats.

Just then, a waiter approaches our table. He stares at us for a few beats, seeming nervous, before speaking. "Um, I'm Jeff," he says. "I'll be taking your order."

LOS ANGELES TRAVEL *Design*

CM CM

STRIPED
LONG-SLEEVED
T-SHIRT

SUNGLASSES

GOLD
BRACELET

YELLOW
SANDALS

RIPPED
JEANS

"Hi Jeff," says my mom warmly. "We'll both be having the turkey paninis with a side of arugula and goat cheese salad."

Jeff writes the order down, avoiding eye contact. "Anything to drink?" he asks.

"A pink lemonade for each of us," I say.

Jeff looks up at me, then quickly back at his pad of paper. "Thank you," he mumbles before going back inside the restaurant.

"Do I have food stuck in my teeth or something?" I ask my mom, smiling wide.

"Nope. I just think you're wrong about your fifteen minutes being up," she replies. "He probably recognizes you from *Teen Design Diva*."

I wave my hand dismissively. "This is LA. There are way bigger celebs here." To prove my point, I glance around the restaurant, but I can't see who's who beneath any of the pastel-colored umbrellas.

Mom shrugs. "True, but reality shows are hot. Plus your face is still memorable thanks to your guest judging appearance on *Teen Design Diva* this past season. The producers wouldn't ask you to guest judge again if they didn't think it would be good for the show's ratings."

I groan. I have mixed feelings about my celebrity status. On the one hand, the guest judging and all the opportunities I've been given are amazing. But worrying about how I was portrayed while on the show was less than awesome. When *Teen Design Diva* first aired, our school and town were abuzz about Nina and me. I was glad all that died down this year.

"Your salads and paninis," says our waiter, coming back to our table. The plates rattle a little as he sets them down on the pink tablecloth.

"Thank you," I say, smiling.

The server lingers, and I feel weird eating while he's still there. Finally he takes a deep breath and moves closer to our table. "Here's the thing," he whispers after a quick glance behind him, "I'm not allowed to do this, but my girlfriend's birthday is tomorrow. She's a huge fan and loved all your designs on *Design Diva*. She wants to be a designer too. Any chance I can have your autograph? I'd win the prize for best boyfriend ever."

"Sure," I say with a smile. "No problem. I'll sketch something and sign it for her before we go."

"Thanks so much!" He hurries off to wait on another table.

Mom gives me an *I-told-you-so* look. "As I was saying . . ."

"Yeah, yeah." I bite into my sandwich, feeling happy and flattered. Sometimes being recognized isn't so bad after all.

"Welcome to FIDM!" our perky tour guide says later that afternoon. "My name is Claire, and I'm a senior. Today, I'll be your eyes and ears for everything FIDM. If you have any questions, feel free to ask."

My mom and I — along with a dozen or so prospective students and their parents — are gathered at the entrance to FIDM's campus. The white buildings serve as a good contrast to the colorful shrubs and grassy area situated before them. If a campus could feel fashion-forward, that's how I'd describe this one.

Claire's outfit doesn't disappoint, either. She's paired a pleated white top with black stretchy jeans and black ankle boots. A red leather jacket adds a pop of color and fun accessories complete her look.

TOUR GUIDE OUTFIT Design

WHITE PLEATED CAMI

RED LEATHER JACKET

BLACK SKINNY JEANS

BLACK BOOTIES

"This is the main reception area," Claire continues, leading us into a room with art deco style carpet, muted lighting, and comfy-looking furniture. The students sitting on the couches and chairs are playing on their phones or sketching. In the middle of the room is a mannequin dressed in a patterned shift dress.

"Even the reception area is fashionable," I whisper to my mom. Just like that, I can picture myself here. It's silly because I've only seen the courtyard and this one room, but for once, I let myself enjoy the feeling and push the what-ifs out of my head.

"What I love most about FIDM is the atmosphere," Claire tells the group. A group of students walks by, and Claire gives them a discreet wave. "You're so close to all the entertainment and fashion events, and that excitement transfers to the building and the classes."

A girl wearing loose peach-colored jogger pants and a black-and-white sweater raises her hand. "Um, how do you focus on school here? It seems so fun and exciting."

Claire laughs. "I felt the same way when I first started here, but you get used to it. Even as a senior, I find this place amazing. But you remember why you came here, which is to be a designer, and you put the fun to the side."

The girl nods, but the look on her face tells me she's not convinced.

"Let's keep walking," says Claire. "The classrooms are next."

The classrooms are just as cool as the reception area. Everything is brightly colored, and there are several mannequins stationed around the room for the students to work on too. If we had these kinds of classrooms at my school in Santa Cruz, no one would ever complain about going to class.

The other prospective students in the group whisper things like "cool" and "awesome," and Claire tells the group, "The goal of FIDM's classes is not only to teach but to inspire as well."

Okay, that sounds totally cheesy and like something all the tour guides have to say, but it seems true too. Unlike in my school, I don't see anyone in the class playing on his or her phone or hiding behind a book to take a nap. They're all listening to the teacher and cutting and measuring and *smiling*.

"How long are classes?" asks a boy on the tour.

"Each one is three hours long," says Claire. "And carrying a muslin, tote bag, textbooks, and a tool kit to each one can be a pain. You have to plan so you're not late to class."

Three hours? I think. *Sheesh!* The classrooms may look fun, but that's a long time. And, if I'm going to carry all that stuff, I need to start working out now so I don't hurt myself!

Claire leads the group out of the classroom and back down the hall. "These window displays," she says, pointing to a glass case with a dressed mannequin, "are all done by students."

The current mannequin is wearing a strapless multicolored dress. It has a sweetheart neckline and looks like it's made of flowers. I imagine one of my designs showcased like this for everyone to see. It'd be a dream come true.

"Another amazing thing about FIDM is our museum. It's open to the public and totally free," says Claire.

"Unlike this school," a dad in the group jokes.

Claire looks at him and nods. "You're right. This school has so much to offer. The fact that it's so close to the movie and television industry in LA allows FIDM to bring in terrific industry professionals. We also have a great alumni program, and most of our students get jobs after graduation, but this is an expensive school." She looks around and lowers her voice. "There is a lot of opportunity here, but if you're comparing it to some other fashion schools, the price is more than double."

My heart sinks. We're still working out how to pay for transportation to NYC for my FIT and Parsons tours, and that's just two plane tickets. College tuition will cost way more.

My mom looks at my sad face and then at Claire. "But you have programs that can help here, right? Financial aid and things like that?"

"Yes! Definitely." Claire looks relieved that my mom mentioned this. "The financial aid office is a great resource, and we offer scholarships. And students can also work to help pay for their education."

Hearing Claire's assurances makes me feel a little better. I didn't plan on working while I was in college, but it could be an option.

Claire seems eager to change topics to something less stressful. "Let's walk to the museum next," she suggests. "The current exhibit showcases designs from Emmy-nominated shows."

When we enter the museum, I immediately think of all the fashion and entertainment magazines Alex and I read. She would love this place. I even recognize a few dresses from my favorite shows. One is from a creepy series Alex and I watch called *Beneath the Ground*. It takes place in an alternate universe, and the characters wear Victorian-inspired clothing.

I recognize a dress from last season's finale. It's a red-and-white Georgian-style gown in cotton and satin with a matching choker. I take out my sketchpad and do a quick drawing so I don't forget the small details. I want to try and sketch a more modern version when I get home. Out of the corner of my eye, I notice two other students on the tour doing the same. It might sound cheesy, but this makes me feel connected to them and this place even more.

"Our last stop," Claire announces, "is the annex." She leads us back outside to where our tour began. This time we go past the courtyard and enter through the side of the building. "You might recognize this *pool* from our brochures, but it's not really a pool."

I move closer to it. This close, it's easy to see that the pool isn't filled with water after all — it's a sunken area covered with blue mats for lounging and studying. The *pool* is surrounded by a raised platform with laptop-equipped lounge chairs. It's easily the coolest study area I've ever seen.

"Who can see themselves sitting and sketching on these chairs?" Claire asks. We all raise our hands. "Then I've done my job," she says with a smile. "It was great meeting all of you, and I hope you'll apply."

When Claire leaves, my mother and I sit side-by-side on the lounge chairs. There are students around, but they don't seem to mind us being here.

"So what do you think?" Mom asks. "Do you like it?"

MATCHING
CHOKER
NECKLACE

FIDM
MUSEUM
Sketches

LONG &
ELEGANT

TASSEL
CLUTCH

- Victorian-inspired
- Alternate universe
- Creepy TV series
- "Beneath the Ground"

RED
EMBROIDERY

COTTON &
SATIN

I nod, still in awe. "I do. How can you not?"

"Even I wanted to go to school here after that tour," Mom says with a laugh.

"It's way more expensive than FIT, though," I say.

Mom nods in agreement, and I'm glad she doesn't try to sugarcoat anything. "That's something you'll have to think about. If you went here, you'd most likely have to do the work-study program, which might be hard to balance while you're studying."

"True," I say. "Can we maybe think more about that later? Like after I've toured the New York schools? I just want to pretend anything is possible for a little while longer."

Mom smiles. "Sure," she says. "I think you deserve that."

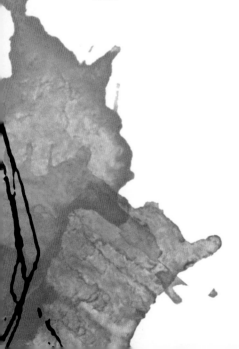

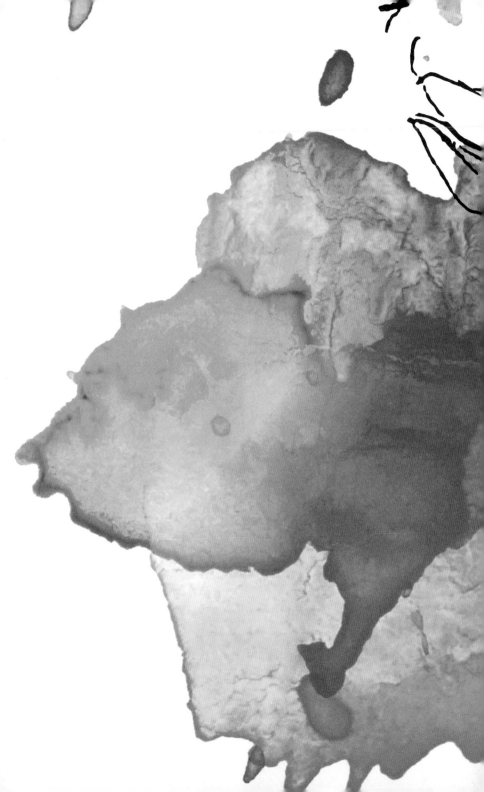

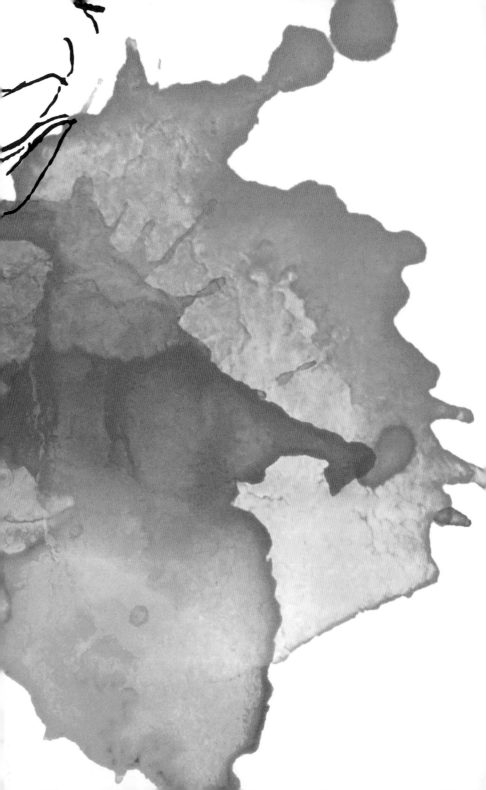

When Monday — the day of my *Teen Design Diva* gig —
rolls around, I can tell my mom is glad it's our last day in
Los Angeles. The rest of the weekend flew by, and I could
happily stay here longer, but the LA noise and activity has
been getting to Mom. She needs a break. She says it's even
worse than New York.

I kind of get what she's saying. There seems to be more
car congestion and traffic here. I'm fine with it, though.
That's what life in the city is like. But thankfully Mom will
have the day to take it easy. She's going to go check out a
cute bookstore she found. It even has a small nook where
customers can curl up on cushions and read.

While Mom is resting, I'll be in the conference room
on the top floor of our hotel acting as guest judge. Just

like during my time at *Teen Design Diva*, the producers are using the hotel to not only house the contestants but also as the workroom and studio for the competition. I wish I knew the theme of today's challenge ahead of time so I could mentally prepare, but I'm guessing they want me to approach the task with fresh eyes.

Since I don't have to be on set for judging for another two hours, I have plenty of time to kill. I start by flipping through the full-color coffee table book in our room. It shows the hotel as it was in its early years, and how it was finally completed in 1925.

Even though it's been updated since then, the current owners have kept key pieces from the original building, including signed photos of famous movie stars. The hotel and our room have a very old-style Hollywood feel. Much of the décor is done in shades of burgundy and gold. Even the walls are burgundy. White moldings form a frame around the ceiling, and decorative gold swirls accent the corners.

I finish flipping through the book and still have plenty of time before I'm due upstairs, so I head down to the lobby. The décor reminds me of the red carpet premieres I've seen on television. There are even velvet ropes in front of the check-in desk, and the walls are covered with black-and-white photos of old movies and movie stars.

I spot an armchair that's off to a corner and sit on it to sketch. I imagine the many people who've passed through this hotel in the past. Just then a woman approaches the front desk to ask about good places to eat. She's wearing a strapless yellow knee-length dress with a ruffle along the bottom hem and red pumps. I pull out my sketchbook and do a quick drawing of her outfit. Her retro look would fit in perfectly with my vision of how the hotel would have looked back in the day.

I like how the woman is dressed, but I decide to play with the design to transform it into something a bit more modern, making it my own. Rather than a retro, feminine dress, I draw a cool, modern jumpsuit, keeping the bright, bold yellow the same on both designs. I sketch quickly, adding a cowl neckline, beaded shoulders, and loose, drapey pants. I imagine the jumpsuit in a luxurious fabric like satin. Paired with a bold lip and a fun, feathered clutch, it would be the perfect outfit for a night out.

I look at the two drawings side-by-side — the retro version and my modern twist — and wonder if there's a way to add this dress to my portfolio. All the schools I'm applying to have different portfolio requirements, and while this doesn't match any of them exactly, maybe there's a way to make it work.

STRAPLESS
SWEETHEART
BODICE

FEATHER
CLUTCH

RUFFLE
HEM

YELLOW
KNEE-LENGTH
DRESS

PANTS &
CAMISOLE
COMBO

RED
SHOES

ORIGINAL
LA HOTEL
Design

I smile. It's been a while since I sketched something just for the sake of sketching. Lately it feels like my portfolio is the only reason I pick up my pencils and sketchpad. It's nice to have it be an afterthought rather than the *reason* I'm designing.

I realize that's one reason this whole college application process has been stressing me out so much. In the past, any time I've been upset, anxious, or overwhelmed, all I had to do was take out my sketchpad and draw something. By the time I was done, the bad feelings would have lessened or disappeared altogether, and I'd be able to face whatever lay ahead.

These days, though, the college clock is ticking, and since each sketch is a portfolio necessity, there hasn't been time to be creative on my own terms. It's been hard to fit in drawing for the sake of drawing. Designing is something I've always loved, but lately it's become work.

I check the clock. The producers don't need me upstairs for another thirty minutes, but I know how cranky Jasmine — one of the *Design Diva* judges — can get when she thinks people are running late. It won't hurt to get there a little early.

I close my sketchpad, feeling lighter than I have in weeks. I remember how stressful being a *Teen Design Diva* contestant was. Maybe part of my role today will be to remind the designers not to forget why they wanted to be on the show in the first place. After all, it never hurts to have a reminder that what someone else thinks shouldn't stop you from following your dream.

16

"There she is!" Missy, another of the *Design Diva* judges,
exclaims as soon as I open the door to the conference room.

I had expected the room to have the same vintage feel
as the rest of the hotel, but it looks more like a huge office.
Even the carpeting is a drab, dark blue. The plus side is that
there is tons of space for the design contestants to stretch
out material and work. That's more important than a pretty
space.

"Chic as usual," says Jasmine, giving me air kisses on
both cheeks.

"Thanks," I say. I try to keep my voice light and casual,
so it doesn't give away the fact that this is the third outfit I
tried on before deciding it was the one. I always feel extra
pressure to look good during *Design Diva* tapings. First,

there's the need to impress the judges. Then, I feel like I have to make a good impression on the contestants. If I don't look like I know what I'm doing as a designer, they'll ignore what I have to say. Last, there's the whole being on television thing.

I once read an article about the dos and don'ts of television appearances, and it gave a whole rundown of best colors to wear. White can make you look too bright, while black can make you look washed out. Patterns appear to vibrate on the screen, and red is a no-no because it bleeds into the screen. Pastels are best.

It was *a lot* of rules to follow, but I worked hard to find the best outfit that was *me* but also worked on screen. The winner was a light blue chambray top with pale pink jeans. Metallic heels add some pizzazz.

"Good to see you, Chloe," Hunter, the final judge, greets me. "We have an interesting challenge ahead of us today. Any guesses as to what it'll be?"

I look around the room for clues. There are sewing machines, mannequins, and rolls of fabric in place. The fabric runs the gamut from solid pastels to prints to bright neon. Even with my experience as a contestant on the show and as a guest judge over the summer, there's still no way to know. The task could be anything. But I know the challenges tend to run in the non-traditional direction.

"Clothing inspired by your favorite prehistoric era?" I guess blindly.

Missy laughs. "Not even we are that out there. Although, maybe we should be."

I think she's kidding at first, but then she takes out a notepad and jots something down.

"I'll give you a hint," Jasmine says. "It has to do with this hotel."

Of course! That would totally make sense. The judges always have a reason for what they do. When I was on *Teen Design Diva*, one task involved cupcakes that were wheeled into the colorful hotel lobby.

"Hollywood-inspired designs?" I guess, thinking of the old Hollywood feel I picked up on earlier.

"Close," Hunter says. "Movie-inspired designs."

"That is fun! And much better than the challenge I had to do with Nina that involved using stuff from the hardware store."

Hunter chuckles. "We felt bad about that — kind of. Speaking of Nina, have you seen her around?"

"We're actually kind of friendly. Weird, right?"

Missy raises an eyebrow at that. "A little, but promise me that when the two of you open your own boutique one day, you'll credit the show for bringing you ladies together."

Now it's my turn to laugh. "I promise. But I don't see that happening."

Just then the doors open, and the contestants start filing in. Is it my imagination or do they look older than the group I competed with? They don't look scared or nervous. I notice no one is hamming for the cameras, either. These contestants look so serious.

"How long have you been taping?" I ask Hunter.

"We're already more than halfway done," he replies. "Today we'll be narrowing the eight contestants down to six."

That means they're only one task away from the top five. At this point, the contestants probably know what to expect. They've probably also realized that even if they do their best, there's no telling what the judges will say.

"What's this group like?" I whisper.

"Very mature," says Missy. "But also very no-nonsense. And they talk back a lot."

"That must be frustrating," I say.

"Sometimes," Missy says, shrugging. "But it makes for good television, and isn't that the point?"

I thought the point was to be the best designer you could be, but I keep that thought to myself.

Jasmine waits for everyone to get settled down. Then, she snaps her fingers and says, "Welcome!"

A girl in a blue baseball cap and overalls actually rolls her eyes. If Jasmine sees this, she ignores it. I look around the room. Some of the designers have their eyes on Jasmine, while others are focused on the floor. A guy in a green fedora and paisley shirt is moving his fingers at his side like he's playing air guitar. A guy in jeans and work boots is scowling at a girl with her hair in braids. Her long-sleeved tee with the word FOOTBALL in the center and black jeans with holes at the knees make me smile. The outfit reminds me of something Alex would have worn once upon a time. She smirks at the guy staring at her, and he scowls and turns away.

"First," Jasmine continues, "let me introduce our guest judge for the day, Chloe Montgomery, the first *Teen Design Diva* winner."

Pigtails Girl smiles at me. Fedora Guy stops playing his imaginary guitar and gives me a look of approval. Baseball Cap girl rolls her eyes again. At least she's consistent. Some of the contestants clap, while the rest look like they couldn't care less that I'm here. Maybe they don't.

The reaction makes me nervous, like I have to prove myself once again. I know it's silly. I'm just here to help; I don't have to put on some show. But I can't help it. Maybe it's the all-too-familiar environment, but it's like I'm back on the show as a contestant again and stuck trying to make people believe I belong.

Hunter motions to a box wrapped in gold paper that's sitting on a nearby table. "You will each pick a slip of paper from this box," he says. "It will tell you a movie title. Your job will be to create an outfit inspired by the movie you've chosen. Volunteers to go first?"

Baseball Cap waves her hand in the air. For a change, she's alert and interested.

"Tina, come on up," Hunter says to the girl.

Tina runs up, closes her eyes, and puts her hand into the box. "*101 Dalmatians*," she says with a sigh. And it's back to sullen eye rolling.

"Can I go next?" the girl with pigtails asks.

"Here you go, Lexi," says Hunter, shaking the box.

"*The Wizard of Oz!*" Lexi says, clapping her hands.

Fedora Guy — whose name turns out to be Peter — gets *Finding Neverland*, which I think is a good fit. Work Boots — also known as Lee — gets *Men in Black*. The other movies picked are *The Devil Wears Prada*, *Star Wars*, *The Sound of Music*, and *Father of the Bride*.

"You have three hours," Jasmine announces once all the movies are picked. "You may begin."

17

I expect the contestants to make a mad dash for the fabric and sewing machines, but instead they all take out their sketchpads and start drawing.

"Wow," I say. "That's not how everyone reacted during my season."

Missy shrugs. "I guess that's what happens when they've seen two seasons of the show and kind of know what to expect."

"The designs are less entertaining," Jasmine complains, pouting.

"Not good television, huh?" I tease.

"Exactly," says Missy.

The first hour is a little boring with the contestants all sketching and measuring. Just when I think they're cutting it close, they start to gather fabric. Lee starts with black and metallic fabrics, and Peter picks green tulle and lace. Vicki, who got *Star Wars*, chooses muted colors like browns and khakis. Other contestants are clearly going for something a little more glamorous based on the lace, satin, and embellishments they've chosen.

I walk around and am impressed with how quickly the designers are able to sew. I notice Vicki make a mistake with her stitching, but she quickly rips the thread and fixes the problem. The designers use their mannequins efficiently too, draping fabric, measuring there, cutting here, and adjusting the results — all within minutes.

I walk up to Peter and watch him make a belt with the leather, velvet, and gold clasp. Then he uses a sheer fabric to create what looks like a bodice.

"When I saw you choose the materials, I was thinking Peter Pan," I say.

"That would have been too cutesy given my name," he says. "And too obvious given the film. I wanted something a little girlier too since this is my little sister's favorite movie."

"That's really sweet," I say. "Good job so far."

I walk up to Lee. His *Men in Black* inspired design is less than endearing. I love metallic fabrics, but I'm not sure what he's trying to do.

"Can you tell me about your piece?" I ask him.

"Not really," he says. "I mean not now. I don't like to give away what's behind the genius. Trust me, though, you'll be amazed."

"I'll wait to be awed," I say, trying not to laugh as I move on to the other contestants.

The ones that interest me the most are the designs inspired by *The Sound of Music* and *The Devil Wears Prada*. When I pass Nancy, the designer for *The Sound of Music* style, she's working on a white peplum dress. I'm about to ask her more about it, but think about what Lee said and decide that being surprised is not a bad thing.

I move over to Becca's *The Devil Wears Prada* design. It's a little hard to figure out. The fitted sleeveless top has a large bow at the collar that looks odd.

"I'm working on the sleeves," Becca tells me through a mouthful of pins.

"Can't wait to see," I say. I hurry away, afraid she'll choke on the pins if I keep talking with her. I walk around the other designs and wonder which one the judges will like the most.

"One hour!" Hunter announces, but no one seems fazed or hurried.

My phone vibrates, and I look down to see a text from Jake. I know he wants to hear how my FIDM tour went,

135

especially since I told him about my application anxiety last week, but there's a reason I haven't texted him yet. I don't want to tell him that it went great, and I'm loving LA, especially since I know he's hoping I'll come back to New York for college. I'll have to talk to him soon, but not now. At this moment, I need to keep my head in this room.

Just then Hunter calls, "Thirty minutes," and the cameramen converge on the contestants and their designs. Even though the contestants' faces don't show much emotion, I notice beads of sweat on their foreheads. I also see them wring their hands, bite their nails, and play with their hair — all signs they're just as nervous as I was during the judging process.

Hunter, Jasmine, Missy, and I do one last lap around the room. The contestants' attention shifts from their fabric to the clock and back to the fabric as they all hurry to put the finishing touches on their designs.

"I love this last-minute tension," Jasmine says, rubbing her hands.

I frown. "I don't. Their anxiety is actually rubbing off on me. I totally get what they're going through."

"That's why we have you here, Chloe," says Missy. "I used to be the softie, but I'm afraid I've gotten tougher. You help balance things out."

I frown slightly. I guess that's a compliment.

Hunter laughs. "Ignore them. You're just more humane. Like me." But then, in a loud, booming voice that makes me jump, he shouts: "Time's up!"

So much for softer and more humane.

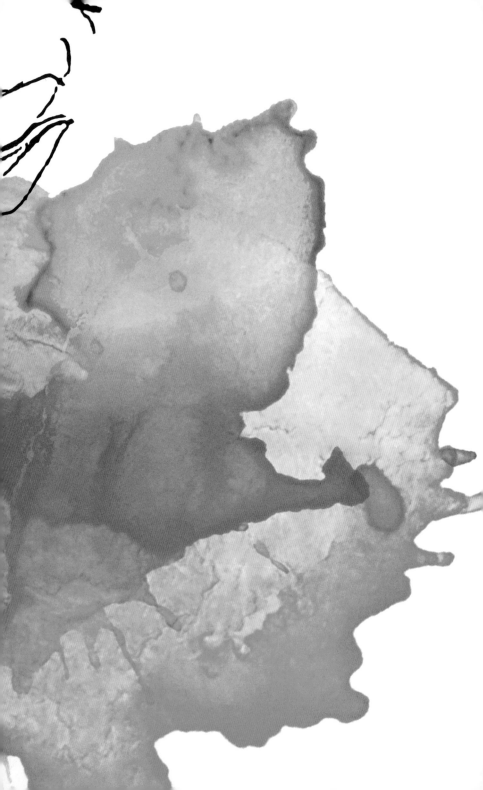

"Lee," says Hunter once all the contestants have gathered in the center of the room with their mannequins, "we'll begin with you. Tell us about your piece."

"Well," Lee starts, "the guys in *Men in Black* were secret government agents, so I thought it would be fun to put a spin on their boring black suits. I chose to create a more modern, feminine version." He points to his fitted sleeveless blazer and ankle-length pants. "I also added a metallic top underneath to give it a futuristic vibe."

"When you said to trust you," I say, "I didn't think you'd come up with a design that's so put-together. Nice job."

Lee gives a slight bow and looks relieved. Vicki's *Star Wars* design is next, and the judges look at each other warily.

CONTESTANT
MOVIE-INSPIRED
Designs

KHAKI
TENT
DRESS

BECCA'S
*THE DEVIL WEARS
PRADA DRESS*

MODERN &
FEMININE
SUITING

BOW
COLLAR,
SWEATER,
& STRIPED
SKIRT

LEE'S
*MEN IN BLACK
SUIT*

VICKI'S
*STAR WARS
DRESS*

"What's your inspiration for this?" Missy finally asks.

Vicki straightens the khaki fabric. "It's a tent dress, modeled after the clothes the little furry Ewoks wore in the *Star Wars* movie. It gives it a modern spin, don't you think?"

Jasmine purses her lips. "It looks a little shapeless to me."

"I'm really sorry, Vicki, but I have to agree," says Hunter. "A tent dress can look modern and stylish, but it looks like you just pieced the fabric together without really doing measurements."

I want to say something positive, but they're right. There's no definition, and I wonder how this even took her three hours to make.

Fortunately, I'm saved from speaking when Vicki steps back, and the judges call Becca forward. Her finished outfit is glaringly different from what I saw before. The added sleeves complement the bow collar, and she's paired her top with a striped skirt for balance and contrast.

I shoot Becca a discreet thumbs-up, and she smiles. Jasmine makes a few suggestions about better stitching, but even she's stumped to give any other criticism. Lucky for Jasmine, Tina's Cruella De Vil-inspired dress gives Jasmine and the other judges plenty to discuss.

"Notice the contrast of black and white," Tina says, pointing to her dress, which is half-black and half-white.

"The jagged asymmetrical hem is a nod to Cruella's villainous spirit."

"And the high, spiky collar is for the villainous spirit too, I assume?" says Hunter.

"That's correct," says Tina.

"Here's where I'm struggling," says Missy. "The stitching is perfect and professional. The difficulty of the design is impressive too. But I'm just not feeling this dress. It's so over the top."

I think about my goal of keeping the contestants inspired and telling them to stay true to themselves. I open my mouth to say this when Tina stomps her foot.

"Your opinions aren't law, you know," she snaps. "Maybe you just don't get creativity."

Missy grits her teeth. "Our opinions may not be law," she says. "But they decide your fate here."

Tina turns her back to us, and Hunter sighs. "Moving on," he says.

Bubbly Lexi barely lets Missy get the first syllable of her name out before she launches into the description of her Glinda-inspired dress. "For the bodice, I made a plunging V-neck of gathered silk crepe. This is draped into a wide, gathered waistband with an organza bolero jacket," says Lexi.

"It's really lovely," I say. "You did a beautiful job on the skirt as well."

"Thank you," says Lexi. "I imagined Glinda's dramatic entrance and was trying to mimic that drama with the yards of organza gathered and pintucked into a skirt."

"This makes me want to see the movie again," says Missy.

"I'm just glad you didn't do anything wizard- or munchkin-inspired," Jasmine adds.

"Thank you guys so much," gushes Lexi.

"Two more to go," says Hunter. "Peter, you're up."

"Yes, so as I was telling Chloe, I have a sister who loves all things Peter Pan, so she was my inspiration for this dress," says Peter. "She loves lace, flowers, and ruffles, so I included all of those elements in my design."

"The flowers fit beautifully with the tulle," I say.

"And I like its romantic quality," Hunter adds.

Peter grins. "Thank you."

"Finally," says Hunter, "we have Scott with his *Father of the Bride* design."

When I see Scott's finished design I'm both surprised and impressed. I'd never match his design with his current style. Unlike the Yankees jersey, baggy shorts, and high-top sneakers he's wearing, his dress design is both fun and elegant.

"Seems like sisters are the theme of the day," says Scott. "Mine just got engaged and wanted me to design her wedding dress. The movie I got was like, crazy coincidence."

"Totally," says Hunter. "Why the two-piece?"

"My sister isn't super formal, so I wanted something more off-beat but still elegant. I think I did that with the full skirt and lace halter top," says Scott.

"I agree," says Missy. "I hope she likes it."

"Thank you all," says Hunter. "We will let you know our thoughts soon."

As the contestants get a breather, the judges and I head into another room to discuss the designs, although there's not much to discuss. Our favorites are Becca's *The Devil Wears Prada* design, Nancy's *The Sound of Music* inspired dress, Peter's *Finding Neverland* design, Scott's *Father of the Bride* two-piece wedding ensemble, and Lexi's *The Wizard of Oz* Glinda-inspired gown. That leaves Tina's Cruella-inspired dress, Lee's *Men in Black* suit, and Vicki's *Star Wars* sack — I mean dress.

"Well," says Jasmine, "I think we can all agree we have to let Vicki go. That leaves Lee or Tina."

"Tina's was definitely more inspired than Lee's," says Hunter, "but —"

I interrupt. "She's kind of rude, and it seems like she doesn't really want to get better if it means messing with her vision." I learned a lot from my experience on *Teen*

Design Diva and during my internship. It's important to stay true to yourself, but you also have to be willing to see that there might be a better way to do things.

"Exactly," says Hunter. "I'm sure she'll go places, but she's been giving us attitude from day one. This experience is about learning, and it's clear she doesn't think we have anything to teach her."

"I completely agree," Jasmine says, "but every show needs a villain."

"I hear you, Jazz," says Missy, "but I've had enough of her too. At least Lee will take direction, and I know he'll create something more daring next time. We have a situation here where both are talented. I'd rather talk with Lee again."

Jasmine sighs. "You're right, I know. She's gotten on my last nerve too."

"So it's decided," says Hunter.

We all nod and head back in to break the news to the designers. As the producers and cameras get into position for the elimination, I brace myself for Tina's reaction, doubting it will be pretty.

At least it'll be good preparation, I think. Because I'll soon have to tell Jake my own bad news — that after seeing FIDM, I'm not so sure FIT is my only dream school anymore.

CONTESTANT
MOVIE-INSPIRED
Designs

LEXI'S
THE WIZARD OF OZ
DRESS

SILK
CREPE
BODICE

BLACK
BOA

BOLERO
WRAP

DALMATIAN
DOTS!

HI-LOW
HEM

TINA'S
101 DALMATIANS
DRESS

GATHERED
ORGANZA SKIRT

CONTESTANT
MOVIE-INSPIRED
Designs

PETER'S
FINDING NEVERLAND
DRESS

FLOWER
CROWN

FLOWER
DETAILS

LACE
HALTER
TOP

FULL
TAFFETA
SKIRT

GREEN
TULLE &
LACE

GATHERED
SKIRT

OFF-BEAT
& ELEGANT

SCOTT'S
FATHER OF THE BRIDE
DRESS

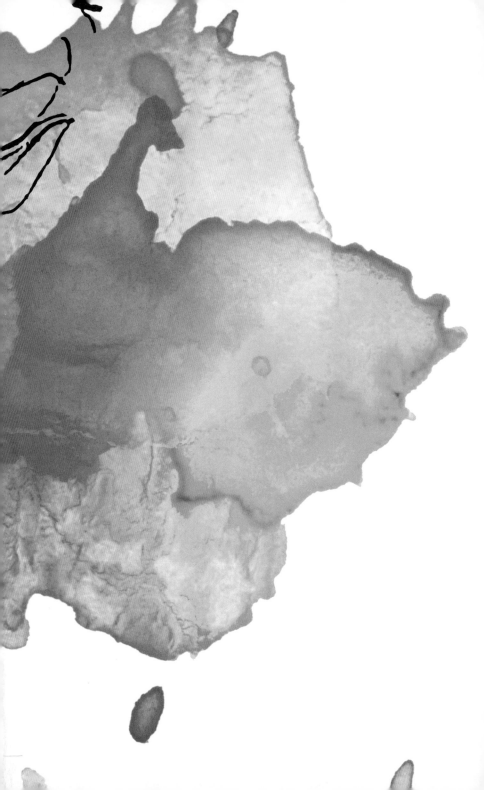

19

"What do you mean you haven't told Jake yet?" Alex asks as we walk through the mall back home later that week.

I admit, I'm kind of being a coward. I've been back in Santa Cruz for three days, and so far all I've told Jake about FIDM is that it was "okay." And even that was through texts.

"I just know he'll be bummed if I tell him how much I liked it," I say. "It's the kind of conversation you want to have with someone in person, you know?"

"True, but when is that happening?" Alex asks. "You can't avoid him forever."

"This weekend, apparently. Liesel is having a fashion show in Santa Cruz, and he's flying in to help her."

Jake's mom, Liesel McKay, is a famous fashion designer and *Design Diva* winner. She even acted as my mentor on the show during my season.

"And you just found out?" asks Alex.

"It was a last-minute decision," I reply. "Jake wanted to surprise me, but I guess he could tell something was up, so he broke down and told me."

"Geez, Chloe, cheer up. It's not the end of the world," Alex says. "First of all, you know Jake just wants you to be happy. Second of all, as much as I'd love for you to choose FIDM, you're still going to tour Parsons and FIT. Who knows what'll happen?"

I give Alex a hug. She always knows what to say. "You're right. My FIDM visit made me feel better about this whole college thing. I feel less out of the loop now. I mean, I'm still no closer to making a decision, but at least it's a start."

"Exactly," Alex agrees. "And in the meantime, we can focus on more fun stuff — like looking for clothes."

We walk into a store that's more Alex's style than mine, but shopping is shopping. I can't complain. After all, a year ago I would have had to drag Alex to the mall.

"What do you think of this?" Alex asks, holding up a knee-length dress with thick peach and white stripes. "Maybe with my brown suede ankle boots?"

"I love that," I agree, marveling at how far Alex's style has come. "You just need the right accessories." I spot a long, gold chain on a jewelry rack and hold it up against the dress. "What do you think?"

"Oh, I love that. You have such a good eye for these things." Alex tosses the dress over her arm and flips through some more hangers.

I smile. "Thanks. It kind of reminds me of going through the racks during my internship. I had to see what went together, why people liked it, stuff like that. Jake went on one of those trips with me. Can't say he loved it, though."

While I'm thinking about him, I decide to text him. I take out my phone and type: *Thinking of you while rack shopping!*

Jake writes back in seconds. *Like in NYC. I'd totally suffer through it again if it meant we could hang out.*

"He's so sweet," Alex says when I show her the text. "You guys will make it work, wherever you go."

"I hope so. But that reminds me — I still need to find a way to pay for my flight to New York. Too bad they're not taping another season of *Design Diva* there," I joke.

"Your dad travels for business," Alex says. "Maybe he has frequent flyer miles or something."

"Maybe," I say, but I'm not as optimistic as Alex about it.

"Well, if there's one thing you've shown me, Chloe Montgomery, it's how hard you work at something you want," Alex says with a grin.

I laugh. "That is true. Speaking of, I *want* to see what Bloomingdale's has on sale." I pull Alex into the store and head for the dress section.

"What about this?" asks Alex, holding up a cute A-line dress with lots of flowers.

I shake my head no. "It's pretty, but too flowery for me. It's kind of a Nina dress."

Alex makes a face and puts the dress back on the rack. She slaps her forehead. "Oh! I forgot to tell you. She's been asking about you."

My stomach jumps. "What now? I thought she and I had moved on."

"I don't think it's bad. She said something about college applications. She seemed frazzled. Honestly, I kind of tuned her out."

I frown. "Nice, Alex. It wouldn't kill you to give her a chance, you know. People change."

Alex raises an eyebrow. "Says the girl whose first reaction was 'what now?' when I mentioned Nina's name?"

I hold up my hands in surrender. "Fine, we'll both work harder at seeing the new Nina. I need to talk to her about the Winter Formal dresses anyway. I'm feeling a little overwhelmed. Those three days in LA really set me back. And then there's the portfolio stuff on top of that. Lots of pressure."

"You'll get it all done," Alex says confidently. She picks up another dress off the rack. It's a black, off-the-shoulder, A-line dress that hits at the knee. "This one is definitely you."

I love it. "It would look cute with my chunky black sandals."

"With this chain," says Alex, grabbing a silver necklace off a display.

"Done! Maybe this will be my outfit for Liesel's show," I say. "Jake got me a ticket."

"Maybe you can swing an extra ticket for your BFF?" Alex nudges me with her elbow.

I put my arm around her. "Not this time, I'm afraid. Besides, Jake and I have to talk."

"Riiight," says Alex. "Well, when you're famous, I expect to have a ticket to all your shows."

I pretend to think about it. "If you're lucky."

ALEX'S DRESS SHOPPING *Designs*

SWEETHEART NECKLINE

SKINNY STRAPS

PEACH & WHITE STRIPES

FULL SKIRT

BROWN SUEDE ANKLE BOOTS

PINK FLORAL PATTERN

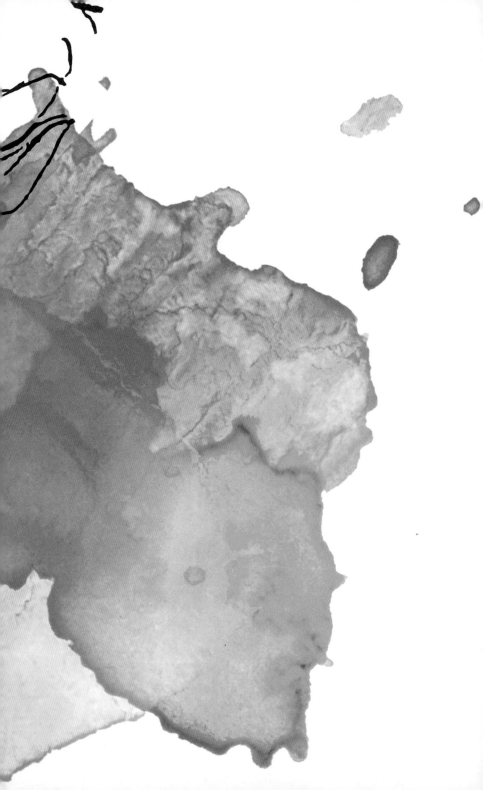

"Chloe!" Liesel exclaims when I arrive at the fashion show venue — an industrial-looking loft — on Saturday. "It's so wonderful to see you again!" She stops making last-minute adjustments on one of the models and hurries over to give me a quick hug.

"Same here," I say, hugging her back. "Thanks so much for inviting me. Jake said the theme is *biker ballerina*? That sounds so interesting! I'm not really sure what to expect."

"Well, I have to admit, I'm glad you can't quite picture it. That way when you see the designs you'll have an entirely fresh perspective."

I laugh. "Fair enough. Have you seen Jake? I'm supposed to be meeting him here."

As if on cue, Jake comes around a corner. When I see him, I can feel my whole face brighten, and I give him an excited wave.

Jake grins and walks over, sweeping me up in a hug. "I can't believe I'm finally seeing you in person!" he says when he pulls back.

I blush. "I know. It feels like it's been forever."

Just then the lights flash off and on. "Well, that's my cue," Liesel says. "You two better get to your seats. See you soon! Enjoy!"

Liesel hurries back to her models, and Jake takes my hand. My stomach gets butterflies. It's been so long since he's held my hand. The way we left things in New York was with the understanding that the time wasn't right for us then. But holding Jake's hand reminds me how much I've missed him.

We hurry to our front-row seats, and the spotlights surrounding the runway flash on. The audience quickly quiets down, and the music cues up. As soon as the first model steps onto the runway, I'm transported to the world of Liesel's fantastic designs. *Biker ballerina* turns out to be a combo of tough and feminine. It's such a great concept. All the designs have an element of leather, and the models' faces are stoic.

As cool as the local fashion show my friends and I atteneded was, this is even better. There's pressure and tension in the air. Photographers are snapping photos from the sides, and the front row is filled with reviewers. It's like the New York hype but in California. Not just in California, but in my hometown.

A model in a brown leather skirt with contrasting blue leather pockets struts down the runway. The skirt is paired with a tight, cropped sweater and strappy sandals. I like the edginess of the look.

The next look is more monochromatic but equally chic. It's a black leather trapeze dress with contrasting piping on the collar and pockets. Liesel has it paired with sandals that lace up to the knee. The dress is both fierce and feminine.

The next model comes out in an outfit that I not only love but could see myself wearing too. It's white and taupe with dark blue accents and eyelet shoulder details. I like the striped pattern, and the blue is a fun, bright pop of color.

"You'd look nice in that," Jake whispers.

"Maybe your mom will give it to me as an early Christmas present," I joke.

"Well, you definitely have the right connections," Jake replies, giving my hand a squeeze.

More models come out, and I'm so impressed with Liesel's range. After she won *Design Diva* several seasons ago, she started a jewelry line. Then, when I was in New York, she collaborated with Stefan on his art deco gowns. And with this new collection, she's showcasing her eye for edgy, feminine style.

LIESEL'S FASHION SHOW *Designs*

MONOCHROMATIC

WHITE PIPING

CROPPED STRIPED SWEATER

BIG POCKETS

LEATHER & SUEDE

LEATHER COLOR-BLOCK SKIRT

LACE-UP STRAPPY HEELS

When I did work for the PR department during my internship, I noticed how easy it was to identify the clothing of some designers. That's not the case with Liesel. It's like she's always reinventing herself. I want to be the same way. I want my designs to keep people guessing.

* * *

After the show, Jake and I congratulate his mom and then head back to my house. Rather than going inside, we take a seat on the porch swing. He hasn't let go of my hand since the show, and I'm glad.

"So it seems like you really liked FIDM, huh?" he says softly.

I look down, avoiding his gaze, and nod. "How did you know?"

"I'm a smart college boy, remember? Not to mention that you managed to answer all of my texts except for the ones about FIDM." He smiles. "It was sort of a dead giveaway."

I sigh. "Picked up on that, did you?"

Jake taps his temple with his finger. "Like I said, smart." We sit quietly for a few minutes, and then he says, "Tell me about the tour, Chloe. I want to hear about it. Seriously."

I smile. Jake is such a good guy. All he wants is for me to be happy. I take a deep breath and tell him all about the tour and the FIDM museum. I talk about the classrooms and how bright and colorful the walls are. I glance over at him when I'm finished and feel better when I see his wide smile.

"It sounds amazing," Jake says. "Now I wish *I* had looked into that school!"

I nod. "I'm glad I saw it. And I'm glad we went to the fashion show today. Both these things made me realize how much California has to offer. I think I kind of wrote it off since I grew up here. But now, even if I do choose New York, I'll at least feel like I gave both options a fair shot."

Jake nods. "That's all you can do. I mean, I'd obviously love it if you came to New York, but you have to do what's best for you."

While I'm in the middle of tackling topics that make me nervous, I might as well bite the bullet — I still need to ask Jake about Winter Formal too.

"Um . . . I also wanted to ask you . . . there's a dance in December," I say. "I know it's a long shot, but do you want to go with me? I mean, that's if you're coming out to Cali to spend the holidays with your dad. Otherwise don't worry about it. I don't want to —"

Jake grins. "I thought you'd never ask," he interrupts.

I'm surprised. "How did you know?"

Jake blushes. "Alex mentioned something about dresses you're designing for the dance online, and . . . I might have looked up your school's website to see when your winter break is. I saw the dance listed on the calendar there. I am coming out here for the holidays, and I had to book my plane tickets and work out details with my dad. But you never mentioned the dance, so I didn't want to push. I thought maybe you wanted to go with someone else."

"Oh my gosh, no! I just didn't know if you'd be able to come." Talk about miscommunication. "Speaking of the dresses I'm designing, did you happen to see that Nina is helping me?"

Jake raises an eyebrow. "Nina? Apparently we have a lot of catching up to do."

"A lot," I say with a smile.

"Let's not get this behind again. I want to know what's going on with you. You can tell me anything."

I squeeze his hand. "Thanks. Same goes for you."

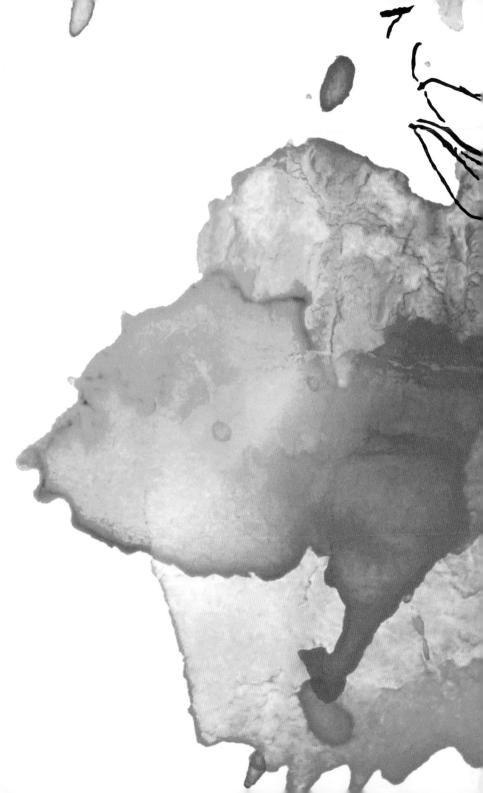

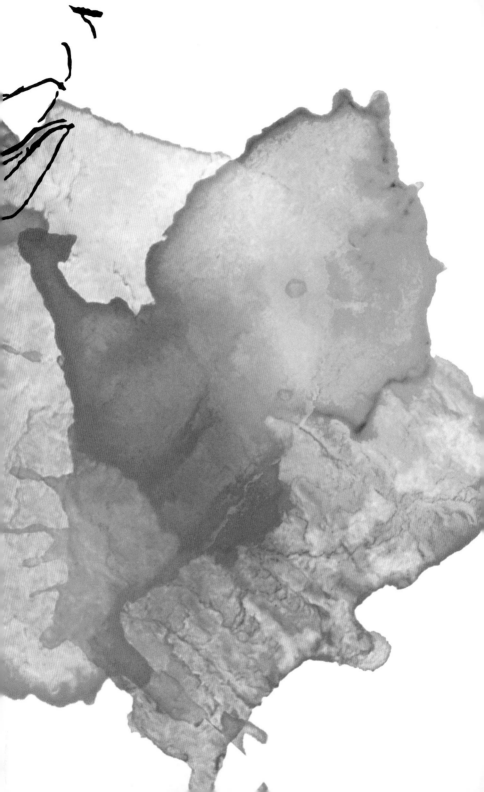

21

"My application is due November first," Jada says at lunch on Monday, "and I don't think I can do it." She's applying for early decision at several Ivy League schools, which means her applications are due almost two months before the rest of ours.

Mia shoots a glance in my direction and shakes her head. Just two weeks ago, I didn't want to hear any college talk — it was too overwhelming. But since I've visited FIDM, I feel better about the whole process.

"Don't worry, Mia," I say. "I'm okay. Besides, if I had something due in two weeks I'd be a real mess."

"Thanks," Jada says with a groan.

"No, I mean I can't believe how well you're handling everything. You seem so calm," I say.

Jada laughs. "It's all on the outside."

"What do you have left to do?" Dan asks. He and Alex are holding hands, as usual. Seeing them together bummed me out when I first came home — I really missed Jake — but after this weekend, their lovey-dovey stuff just makes me smile.

Jada blushes. "Not much. Just sorting my files and uploading them to the right websites."

Mia rolls her eyes. "Sounds like you're done. What's freaking you out?"

"Well," I say, mock seriously, "attaching a document can be hard. What if Jada attaches a clip of puppies instead of her college essay?"

"Yeah," Alex jumps in, "imagine Yale opening the file, and it's a dog chasing a ball. Tricky stuff."

Jada throws a corn chip at Alex. "You guys are the worst!"

"Fine," I say, throwing a chip back at her. "What's really bothering you?"

Jada sighs. "It's kind of stupid, but sending everything in is just so *final*. Does that make sense?"

This time no one teases her. That's something we all get. Even Dan, who's normally goofy, looks a little sad.

"It completely makes sense," says Alex. "It's like we spend all this time working toward this huge thing, and then it's done. Then what?"

"And *then* we have to decide where to go," Mia says. "Ugh, I hate decisions."

"Okay, enough with the depressing big-decision talk," says Dan. "We have the rest of senior year to look forward to. Winter Formal, prom, graduation . . . once college applications are done, it's party time."

"That's another way to look at it," says Jada, smiling again. "Okay, you've convinced me. I'm going home today, attaching documents like crazy, and hitting send."

"That's what I'm talking about," says Dan. "Like a Band-Aid."

I take out my sketchpad to capture this moment of all of us together. I start drawing Alex, who's wearing black leggings, an oversized blouse, a brown scarf, and brown boots. Just last year, those boots would have been sneakers, and she'd never have worn a scarf as an accessory. Then I add Jada's preppier look to the page — a button-down shirt with the sleeves rolled up, blue shorts, and a brown belt.

"Do me next," says Mia, noticing my sketch. She sucks in her cheeks and strikes a pose.

I sketch Mia's ivory tulle skirt, chunky black ankle boots, fitted black shirt, and funky hat.

"Chloe, I'm taking you to New York with me," says Mia, leaning over to admire my finished drawing.

I pause. "You're applying to New York?"

Mia nods. "I just added NYU to my list. I decided I'm definitely majoring in theater, and they have a great program."

"That's great!" I say. I add a mental checkmark to the pro-New York column. I could potentially have another friend there too.

"Can we just pretend for a few minutes that there's no college stuff left to do?" says Jada. "Let's focus on some of that fun stuff Dan was talking about."

For the last few minutes left of lunch, I take Jada's cue. Even though I'm feeling better about my LA versus NYC decision and college stuff, I'd be lying if I said all those things weren't always in the back of my mind. But for now, I hug my friends and pretend none of us have anything left to worry about.

The next day at lunch, I'm sitting in the courtyard waiting for Nina. That morning she appeared at my locker, looking more stressed than I've ever seen her — even taking into account our time on *Teen Design Diva*. She asked if we could meet for lunch, and I agreed. Alex wasn't thrilled I'd be "ditching" her, but I'm hoping she doesn't really see things that way.

"Hey," says Nina, plopping down on the bench beside me. Her hair is all over the place, and her eyes look tired, but her outfit is as stylish as ever. Today, she's wearing a loose gray sweater and a floral skirt. "How was FIDM? We haven't had a chance to talk since you got back."

"It was fantastic," I reply. "I liked it way more than I was expecting to."

"Right? I was so impressed when I visited over the summer." Nina plays with the bracelet on her hand, opens

her lunch, and frowns. "I'm not in a tuna mood. This morning I kind of was, but not now. You have to be in a tuna mood to eat it."

I take a bite of my turkey sandwich, not sure what to say to that. Nina seems all over the place. Tuna mood or not, she unwraps her sandwich and starts to eat. After she doesn't say anything else for five minutes, I say, "So, what's going on?"

Nina groans. "Ugh, sorry. I know I'm being weird. It's just all this application stuff is starting to get to me. I know you felt behind because you hadn't visited schools or started your portfolio, but your real-world experience is kind of intimidating. I was thinking maybe we could help each other."

I almost choke on my sandwich. It's one thing to not hate each other but help? "How would that work exactly?"

Nina looks down and takes a sip of her drink. "I know we weren't exactly friends before, and I —"

"Didn't always play fair?" I interrupt, thinking back to how Nina tried to sabotage me on *Teen Design Diva*.

Nina rolls her eyes. "Fine. Let's say that. But we also pushed each other. We got better because we both wanted to win so badly."

I also wanted to win *fairly*, but I don't harp on that. She's right in a way. I would have preferred Nina not be so obnoxious, but she did make me want to do my best. "Yeah, okay," I say.

"So, here's what I'm thinking — I'm probably ahead of you on the application front, but you can tell me a lot about working in the fashion industry and things you learned from your internship. If we work on our portfolios together, we can bounce ideas off each other." She pauses, puts her sandwich to the side, and picks up her apple.

It's not an idea I would have thought of myself, but I have to admit, it's a good one. I told Alex we need to try to see the new Nina. I'd be a hypocrite if I didn't take my own advice. Besides, it's not a competition like *Teen Design Diva*. If Nina gets into a school, it doesn't mean I won't get into the same one. It's not really a rivalry anymore.

"Deal," I say.

Nina perks up, and she looks much more relaxed than when she first sat down. "Great! There's only ten minutes left of lunch, but I brought some of my Winter Formal designs. I wanted to get your thoughts on them. Then maybe next week you can come over and show me yours and your portfolio too."

"Sounds good," I say as Nina opens her sketchpad.

She flips through the pages. Nina's designs are very pretty but understated. They have elements that stand out, but they're not big on embellishments. The first dress is a

- Textured Bodices
- Floral Accents
- Shades of Plum

NINA'S PORTFOLIO Sketches

FLOOR-LENGTH OMBRÉ GOWN

HALTER BALL GOWN

FLORAL ACCENTS

SILK FABRIC

COCKTAIL DRESS

Nina's Winter Formal ideas

floor-length ombré gown done in silk. Darker shades of plum start at the top and fade into white at the bottom. The bodice is textured and looks like a bunch of flowers sewn together.

I look through more of Nina's pages. Her dresses play with texture and most have a flower motif. I like the variations of floral designs. She even has a few with flowers delicately embroidered into the dress. One of my favorites, not surprisingly, is one without a floral print.

"That one's kind of plain, don't you think?" Nina asks, biting her lip.

I laugh. "I love it. I would totally wear it." The skirt is lavender and a wrap style, and the top is a perfect contrast in a darker purple. She paired it with open-toed shoes in a floral print, which helps break up the solid colors.

Nina laughs too. "I bet we can take each other out of our own comfort zones more."

By the time the lunch bell rings, Nina is smiling. I realize I am too and have been for most of lunch period. It's been a week of surprises. LA was as great as New York. Talking with Jake wasn't as scary as I'd built it up to be. And now it seems I'm bonding with someone totally unexpected. Whatever happens next, I have a feeling there will be more surprises in store.

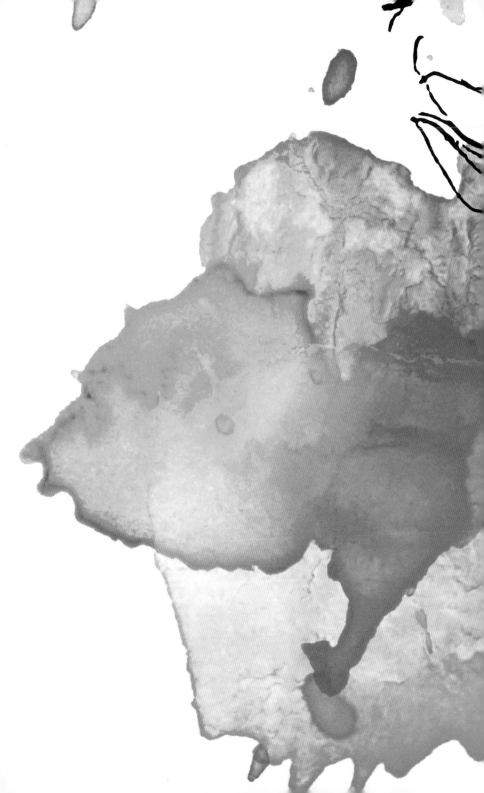

Dear Diary,

Not to toot my own horn, but I think I'm really getting the hang of this college application thing. There are still a lot of portfolio requirements to complete, but I'm actually starting to feel like I'll get them all done. Believe it or not, I have Nina to thank for that. Trust me, I'm as shocked as anyone, but it's been a nice surprise. Brainstorming ideas with someone who's in the same boat has been really helpful.

It's also helped to have someone to talk to about the different schools. Visiting FIDM was better than I imagined, but also threw me for a little loop. I could really imagine myself there. But liking the school — and LA — more than I expected to means I'm going to have an even harder decision to make when it comes to deciding where I want to go to college.

Speaking of . . . in just one week, I'll be back in New York City visiting FIT and Parsons. Dad's frequent flyer miles couldn't cover Mom's ticket *and* mine, but they did pay for one of us. And Bailey, my suitemate from my summer internship, said I could stay in the FIT dorms with her. I know I stayed in the dorms during my internship, but this will be different. I'll get to see what it's like to actually *live* on campus during the school year. I'm also planning to stop by the Stefan Meyers headquarters while I'm in town and see Laura, my former supervisor. Jake and I are trying to make plans to connect too. It should be a great time!

The only thing *not* so great lately is how Alex has been acting. She was in a great mood when I told her how much I loved FIDM. I know she's rooting for me to go there because it's close to UCLA, which is where she wants to go to school. But she also said she just wants me to be happy. I believe her, but every time I bring up my upcoming New York tours, she acts distant and snippy. The fact that I've been spending more time with Nina working on college applications hasn't been helping. Alex is *not* a Nina fan. But Alex also knows she's my BFF — nothing is going to change that. So here's to hoping we can get past this difference of opinions sooner rather than later . . .

Xoxo — Chloe

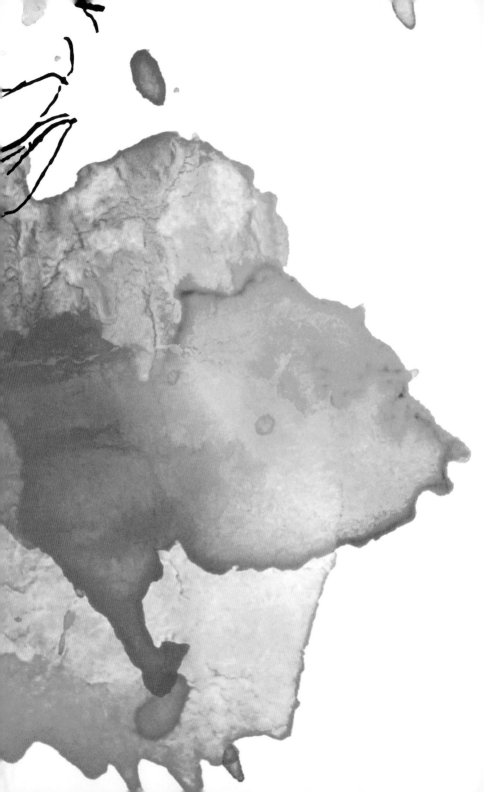

23

"Tell me why we're doing this again," Nina says on Monday after school as she spreads her designs out across her bedroom floor.

I let out a little laugh as I organize my own designs and place them in piles beside Nina's. She and I have a version of this conversation almost every time we get together — which is *a lot* lately. Sometimes I'm the one asking for reminders. Other times it's Nina. It's kind of a running joke now.

"Because we want to get into awesome fashion colleges so we can be fabulous fashion designers," I remind her.

"Riiight," says Nina. "I remember now." She pauses to take in the mess surrounding us on the floor and lets out a sigh. "I just wish the path was a little easier."

I laugh. "Don't we all?"

Today, I brought my pop star designs, one of the requirements for FIT. I have to create a fashion line that imagines what a performer might wear on stage, out with friends, and lounging around. I chose Lola James, one of my favorite singers. So far I think my designs are developing nicely, but the casual wear is looking a little drab. I can't quite figure out what would make them pop.

I pick three looks to show to Nina, putting my least favorite on the bottom of the pile. "What do you think?"

Nina looks at the first sketch, which features an outfit Lola would wear onstage. It's a short silver dress covered in fringe and beading. Sequins embellish the V-neck, and black beads are placed within the silver to break up the colors.

"I like this a lot," she says, holding the sketch at a slight distance to get a better look. "I went to her concert once. She wore this black, sequined outfit, which was fine — very Lola James. I mean, she couldn't look bad if she tried, but *this* is way better. I can imagine it sparkling under the lights. You should send it to her."

I laugh and roll my eyes. "Yeah, right. Picture how that would go."

Nina shrugs. "You never know. Besides," she mumbles, "I'm planning to send my designs to Diana Gardo."

She kind of muffles the last part of that sentence, but I hear her anyway. "Really?" I ask. Diana Gardo is at least as big a star as Lola James. I'd be intimidated to send her any of my work.

Nina looks down and plays with her hair, avoiding eye contact. "Why not? What's the worst that can happen?"

That's the thing about Nina — she's bold. She's not scared of rejection or taking chances, no matter what the results. Alex is like that too. I'm way more cautious, but I know it wouldn't kill me to take more risks.

"You're right," I agree. "It can't hurt."

Nina smiles and looks at my next design — Lola's going-out look. I made the dress electric blue to show Lola's confidence. The formfitting style hits at the knee and is covered in circular and rectangular patterns that remind me of the art deco line Stefan showcased at Fashion Week this past fall. Illusion netting offsets the blue and offers a glimpse of skin.

"This one is hot!" says Nina. "Really different from your usual designs."

My face flushes. "What's that supposed to mean?" I thought Nina and I were finally becoming friends, and then she gives me a backhanded compliment.

Nina shakes her head and puts up her hands, surrender style. "That came out wrong. I didn't mean your designs

CHLOE'S POP STAR *Design*

BEADED DETAILING

SILVER & BLACK FRINGE SKIRT

LOW V-NECK

SILVER MINI DRESS

LACE-UP STILETTOS

FIT PORTFOLIO: *Outfit for stage performance*

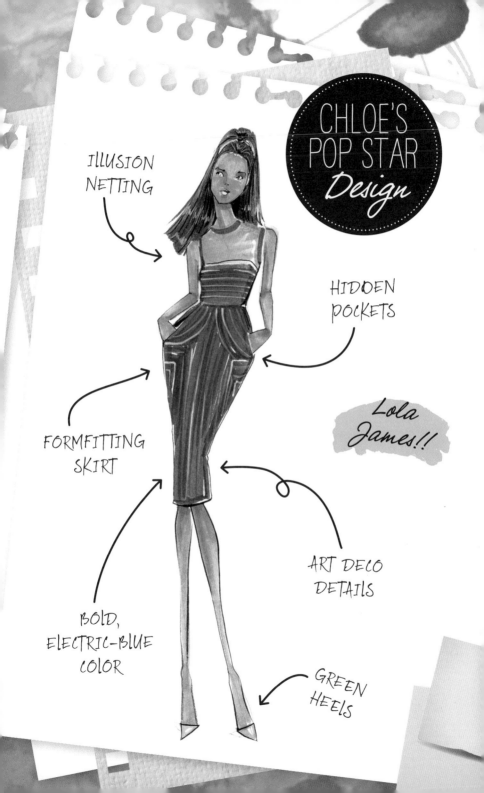

ILLUSION NETTING

CHLOE'S POP STAR *Design*

HIDDEN POCKETS

Lola James!!

FORMFITTING SKIRT

BOLD, ELECTRIC-BLUE COLOR

ART DECO DETAILS

GREEN HEELS

aren't normally hot. I just mean this is edgier than what you usually do." She covers her face. "Ugh. Was that rude too?"

I look at the design. I let myself be more open in that sketch rather than playing it safe. "No, it wasn't rude. You're right. This was a good requirement because it pushed me out of my comfort zone. Lola's style is louder than mine, and I'm glad I got it right."

Finally, Nina looks at my last sketch. For all the edge the first two had, the last has none. This was supposed to be an outfit Lola would wear at home or running errands, so it can't be fancy, but I still want it to be reflective of her personal style. I sketched an easy long-sleeved shirt with black-and-white stripes, black skinny jeans, and gold flats. I also sketched my model with a long fishtail braid and added a gold headband for a little extra sparkle.

"I like the gold," I say, "but I need something to make it less boring."

"This is just Lola picking up groceries or something, right? She doesn't need to be that fancy," says Nina.

"I know, but I still feel like something is missing. Like you said, Lola James probably couldn't look bad if she tried, but this outfit doesn't really have that spark. You know what I mean?"

Nina nods. "Got it. What if you made her pants red and added a black pocket to her shirt to break up the stripes?"

"That's it!" I say. "It was too monochomatic. I can add a red bag for more color, too. Thanks, Nina!"

"No problem," says Nina. "Sometimes all you need is a fresh set of eyes. I have the same problem with some of my designs. Even if the answer is something obvious, I can stare at them forever and still not see it."

"Good thing I'm here then," I say. Again, I think about how much Nina reminds me of Alex sometimes. I can think of several times when I couldn't quite figure out why an outfit wasn't working. Then, Alex would come over, rummage in my closet for a minute, and find the perfect belt or accessory that would make all the difference. Sometimes, at least in my case, a designer can be too close to an idea to see what needs to be fixed.

As if Alex knows I'm thinking about her, my phone pings just then with a text from her asking if we're still on for pizza tonight. I feel Nina watching me as I type my reply.

"You have to go?" Nina asks. She looks a little disappointed but is trying to hide it.

"Soon." I really want to ask her to come with us. The more time I spend with Nina, the more I think she and Alex would get along if they gave each other a chance. "We still have some time, though. Want me to look at your pop star designs?"

NINA'S POP STAR *Design*

EXTREME V-NECK

BLACK LACE-UP SHIRT

STUDDED DETAILS

SILVER PANTS

BLACK HEELS

FLARED HEMS

Nina starts gathering her papers like she's going to put them away. "You don't have to."

"C'mon, we're helping each other, remember? I *want* to."

"Okay," Nina says quietly. I realize it must be a new experience for her to trust me too. She looks through her sketches again for a moment and then reluctantly hands me three designs.

The first image is very rock star. Nina drew silver metallic pants with studs down the side. The top is black with a plunging neckline and lattice lace-up front. The sides have lattice lace-up, too.

"Is it too out there?" Nina asks. "I really wanted to push my limits to show my range as a designer. I know a lot of my stuff is more feminine. I wanted to prove I can do more than that."

"Not at all!" I say. "This is definitely Diana's look. I like how you do edgy."

"It was hard for me, actually," says Nina. "I kept wanting to add a floral pattern, but then it wouldn't have been Diana." She pauses. "Remember when I sent Sophia over for her dress design?"

"Yep," I say, rolling my eyes. "Her design ideas were all over the place. I was convinced you sent her just to mess with me."

Nina grins. "Well, maybe a little," she says. "But it was mostly because I didn't trust myself to create what she wanted. This portfolio piece showed me how to put aside my own vision and work for the client."

I nod and flip to Nina's next drawing. It's a sketch of Diana out on the town with friends. She kept the same rock star motif, but toned it down a bit. Diana still stands out, though, in a modern purple jumpsuit and leather jacket. The jacket has studs accentuating the oversized collar.

"You got to do your purple thing here," I say, taking note of Nina's signature color. "It's a nice way of combining your style sense with hers."

"I was going to do it all in black first, but thought I'd give color a shot. I'm afraid it's a little much, though."

I take a closer look. For Lola James, it might definitely be too much, but it works for the pop star Nina chose. "The lavender softens the sketch. I like it."

Just then, my phone pings a reminder. If I'm going to meet Alex on time, I'd better get going. "Next time I want to see your last Diana sketch," I say.

"You got it," Nina agrees with a smile. This time, I can tell she believes me.

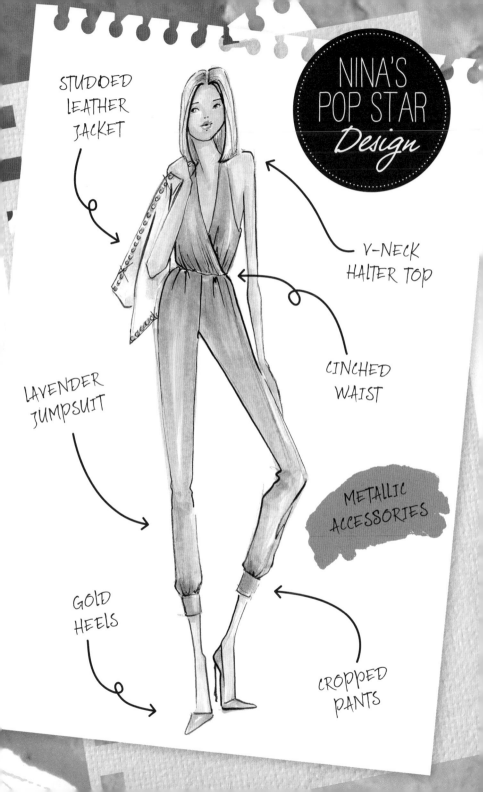

24

"I'm really going to miss hanging out with you like this," Alex says later that week.

She and I are sitting in my room waiting for another classmate/client to arrive to talk about her dress for Winter Formal. With the dance only a few weeks away, I only have time to take on two more dresses. Otherwise, Mimi won't have enough time to sew them.

"It's not like we're not going to hang out once the dresses are done. We see each other all the time." I give her hand a squeeze.

Alex chews on her lip. "Not all the time," she mutters under her breath.

I know what Alex means, but I'm getting a little tired of having this conversation over and over again. When we went out for pizza on Monday, I told her a little about how Nina helped me with my Lola James sketch. Alex just pursed her lips and said something about how I shouldn't be so quick to trust Nina.

I know where she's coming from — Nina wasn't always trustworthy in the past — but I really feel like things are different now. When Alex makes snide comments about Nina, it makes me feel like Clueless Chloe — like I'm someone who needs babysitting because she can't figure things out for herself.

"You're right — not all the time," I say. "There are times you hang out with Dan too."

"That's totally different," Alex protests. "Dan is my boyfriend."

I raise my eyebrows. "So, it's fine for you to hang out with Dan — without me — but it's not okay for me to hang out with Nina and do college stuff? Really, Alex?"

Alex sighs. "I don't know why it bothers me so much. It just does."

I fight back a sigh. I just wish Alex could be happy for me, rather than acting jealous that I've made a new friend. "You're still my best friend," I reassure her. "Nothing's going to change that."

"I know that," Alex insists, but she looks relieved to hear me say it.

I get my sketchpad ready, happy to change the topic. "So who are we waiting for today?"

Alex checks her notes, flipping through a few pages until she gets to the schedule she set up. "Rhiannon Whitman."

I frown. "I don't think I know her. Do you?"

Alex shakes her head. "The name sounds familiar, but I don't *know* her know her. She might have been in my gym class last year."

Just then there's a knock on my door, and my mom pokes her head inside. "Ladies," she says, half-bowing. She always makes a production each time we get a new client. "Rhiannon is here."

A tall, curvy girl with her hair pulled back in a tight bun enters the room. Her boot-cut jeans flatter her figure, and she's paired them with a black tunic top that has embellishments around the scooped neck.

I thought I'd recognize her once I saw her, but she looks only vaguely familiar. Still, I greet her with a smile. "Hi, Rhiannon," I say.

She smiles a warm, open smile. "Hey! I'm so excited about this. My band friends aren't that into fashion, but I love *Design Diva*."

When I hear the word *band*, something clicks. "You play French horn! I remember the last concert. You were great!"

Rhiannon smiles again. "Thanks so much! I love playing, but our band outfits are not exactly fashionable if you know what I mean."

I nod. The marching band outfits are black polyester pants with red shirts. Brass buttons run vertically down the fronts of the shirts and the sides of the pants. The band members also wear matching fuzzy hats. The concert outfits fall on the other extreme. They're very simple — black bottoms and white tops. The girls usually wear a pencil skirt and white blouse.

"So what are you looking for today?" I ask.

"Well, I love metallics," says Rhiannon.

"Great! How about the style? Are you thinking floor-length or short?"

Rhiannon shows me some pictures she ripped out of a magazine. "I like these, but I'd like something floor length. And I think I want something formfitting to accentuate my curves."

I get an idea in my head and do a sketch. I really enjoyed designing some of the more traditional, princess-inspired dresses I've worked on up to this point, but I like the challenge of this one. I envision a slinky, sleeveless metallic wrap dress with a gathered waistband. Maybe something with a long, dramatic train. Rhiannon peeks over my shoulder as I sketch.

"What do you think?" I ask.

"The metallic fabric and the fit are definitely what I had in mind, but I'm not totally sure on the train," Rhiannon says. "I feel like I might spend the whole night tripping over it."

I nod in understanding. The train would be perfect for the red carpet, but I can see how it might be a little much for a high school dance. It's hard sometimes to not get caught up in a design just because I like it. I have to remember to take the client's needs — and the occasion — into account as well.

I get busy shortening the train slightly, adjusting the skirt to a more manageable mermaid draped hem. When I'm finished adjusting the hem, I add a cool bow flounce at the hip to balance the silhouette.

"How's this?" I ask, moving my sketchpad closer to Rhiannon.

"That's perfect," Rhiannon gushes. "You *are* a genius, just like everyone's been saying."

Alex grins. "That's Chloe!"

"Stop it, you two." I feel my cheeks flush. "But I'm so glad you like it."

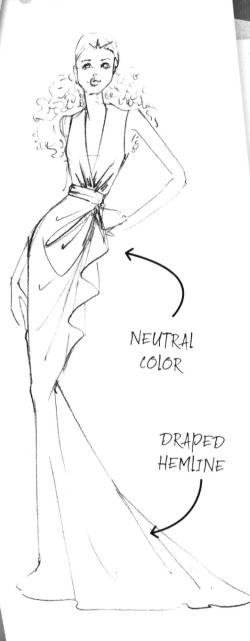

NEUTRAL
COLOR

BOW
FLOUNCE

DRAPED
HEMLINE

To Do:
Winter Formal
designs for
classmates

"Not like," says Rhiannon. "Love!"

I give Rhiannon Mimi's info so she can get the dress made, and the smile is still on my face after she leaves. "This has been so fun," I tell Alex. "I've felt like I've been living my dream of being a real fashion designer."

"I know! It's been a blast," says Alex, but she doesn't look happy — she looks worried. "But I just realized something. We have a problem."

"What do you mean?" I ask.

"Chloe, we've been so busy planning all the other girls' dresses, we've totally forgotten about our own!"

"What?" I ask. "How is that possible?" I look through my sketchpad, hoping something will magically appear. But Alex is right. "Oh, man."

"Do you think Mimi can fit both of us in?" asks Alex, sounding a little unsure.

"I hope so," I say. "We're going to feel pretty silly if everyone else has amazing dresses, and we're wearing something off the rack. I'll call Mimi later and ask. Then I just have to design something. No pressure there."

Alex's eyes light up. "I just got the best idea! You know me perfectly, and I totally trust you. Can my dress design be a surprise?"

I shoot her a look. "I'm flattered, but do you really think that's a good idea? You've seen the girls who came in here. Even the ones who knew what they wanted had trouble narrowing down the design."

"That's just the thing. This will take all the back-and-forth out of it." Alex clasps her hands together in a begging position. "Please? I want to be surprised."

I have to admit, it *would* be fun to design something for Alex. And I'm already using her clothing evolution for my portfolio. This would be a great addition. "Okay," I agree, "I'll do it!"

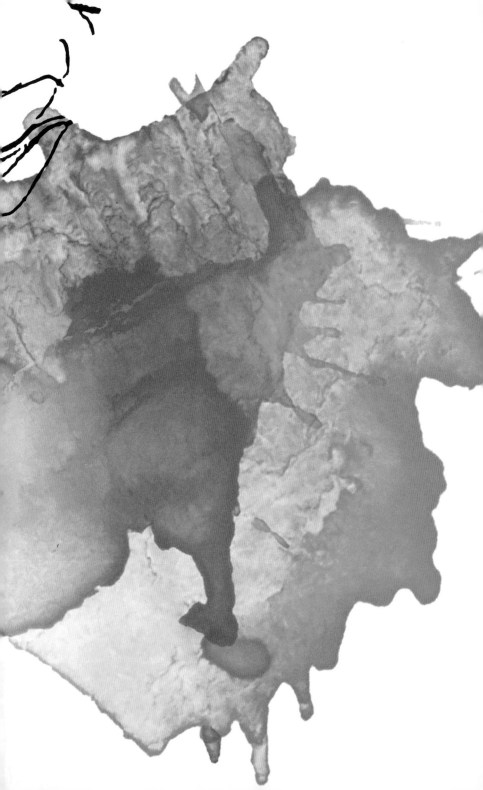

Dear Bailey,

I can't believe I'll be seeing you in exactly one week! Thanks again for letting me stay with you. Bummer that you have a big test on Tuesday, but at least it will be over by the time I get there Saturday! You're too sweet to offer to let me stay Friday and Sunday night too, but Saturday is generous enough. Don't want you getting sick of me! I'll crash with my mom at the hotel the other nights. Thanks again! See you soon!

xoxo

— Chloe

I look over my email to Bailey and hit send. Just thinking about going back to New York makes me so happy. There's something about walking those city streets. I run downstairs to discuss more with my mom and find her sitting at the kitchen table, spiral notebook out. Beside her are five different colored markers.

"What are you doing?" I ask.

"I just want to make sure we don't forget anything," Mom replies, tapping a pink marker on the table and reviewing her notes.

"For when we leave on *Friday*? As in six days from now?" I ask. Talk about over-planning. But I'm not really surprised. Big cities tend to stress my mom out a little. She stayed in New York City with me when I filmed *Teen Design Diva*, so she's a little more comfortable there, but that's not really saying much. Making lists makes her feel more in control.

I don't really have room to judge, though. I'm the same way! I've been making pro/con lists for all my college stuff. And I did the same thing when I was planning my designs on *Teen Design Diva*. It's just easier for me to think when things are laid out in front of me.

I take a peek at my mom's list. She has the things she's packing in one color, the dates of our college tours in another, my visit to Stefan Meyers headquarters and meeting with Laura in a third, and dinner on Friday in another color.

"Looks good," I say. "Maybe I should start thinking about what I'm bringing too." My list, though, will look nothing like Mom's. I like to spell things out in sketches.

"Your way is more fun. If I could draw more than a stick figure, I'd do the same." Mom highlights Friday's dinner in yellow and underlines the Parsons tour in pink. "Are we meeting up with Jake or Liesel at all while we're there?"

"That's the plan," I say, "but we're still trying to figure out a day that works." I'm so excited to see both of them.

Mom looks at her schedule. "Well, let me know what you decide. I need to color-code them."

"Of course you do," I say, resisting the urge to roll my eyes. "All your colors gave me an idea, though. Do I have time to do some sketches before dinner?"

Mom looks at the clock. "Dinner? Shoot. I should probably start that."

"I'll take that as a yes," I say, smiling.

I leave Mom downstairs working on her color organization and head to my room to work on my portfolio. One set of portfolio requirements I've been a little behind on is the swimwear. The idea of doing swimsuits for a seasonal fashion line came quickly to me when I was reading the FIDM requirements, but other than choosing my first three designs, I've done nothing. My mom's color bonanza got my brain moving in that direction again.

I pull out the design I like best. It's a blue-and-neon yellow swimsuit with molded cups and seams, made of scuba material. The midsection of the swimsuit is a lighter blue, but the cups and sides are accented with darker navy blue and neon yellow. It's an adorable swimsuit — if I do say so myself! — but the next step is converting this design to eveningwear.

I start sketching, trying out different lengths and designs, and use shading to play with the textures. I'd like to keep the color scheme the same because it would make a bold statement. With my own clothing, I prefer pops of color. But bolder might be better for this assignment. I envision the bathing suit transforming into a short, body-conscious dress. I use the molded cups for the bodice. Can the dress be in a scuba-type material too? I draw the bathing suit on one side of my sketchpad and the transformation into a dress on the other.

I'm feeling really good about the design and decide to tackle another bathing suit idea while I'm on a roll. My next idea is for a retro-inspired swimsuit. I already drew a red halter top with a sweetheart neckline and adjustable

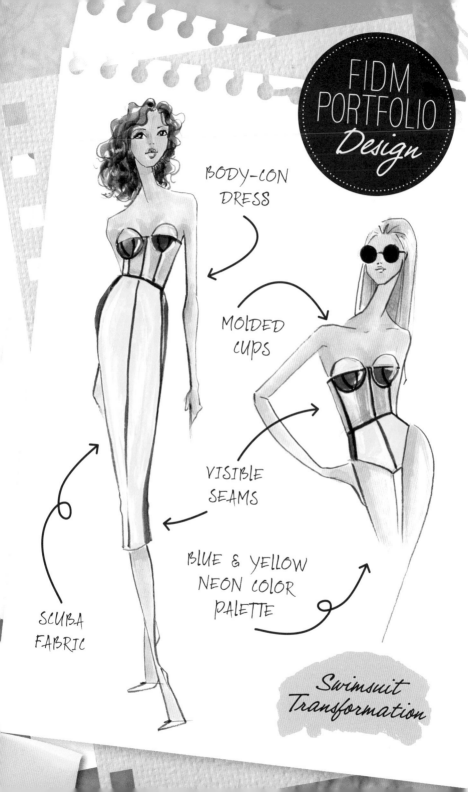

FIDM
PORTFOLIO
Design

BODY-CON
DRESS

MOLDED
CUPS

VISIBLE
SEAMS

BLUE & YELLOW
NEON COLOR
PALETTE

SCUBA
FABRIC

*Swimsuit
Transformation*

straps and paired it with red high-waist bottoms. The red is broken up by white polka dots and ruching.

Unlike the first design, I decide my transformation of this piece will be more casual — maybe something to wear out with friends instead of to a formal event. I start sketching, keeping the sweetheart neckline and halter straps intact. Then I add ruching to the formfitting top and let the skirt flare out at the waist. The red-and-white polka dots give the dress a fun, playful vibe.

I check the clock on my phone. Normally, we'd be having dinner any minute, but given my last conversation with Mom I probably have time for one more design. I flip to my last swimsuit sketch, also a retro look. I drew a white bandeau top with black and white straps and paired it with high-waist, black-and-white striped bottoms. Now I just need to figure out how to transform this design into something unique that can be worn away from the beach.

I get busy drawing bandeau tops and high-waist skirts, trying to find a way to combine both designs in a cohesive way. Something's not working, but I can't quite figure out what. I play with lengthening the skirt, and that does the trick. Next I sketch a white bandeau top and add small straps on the side to connect it to the long, formfitting skirt. A sliver of skin is left exposed where the bandeau top and skirt meet.

"Dinner, Chloe!" Mom hollers from downstairs.

Perfect timing. I close my sketchpad, proud of myself for plowing through this requirement. A few weeks ago, I would have made excuses and decided I didn't have enough time. Today, I didn't let any doubts creep in.

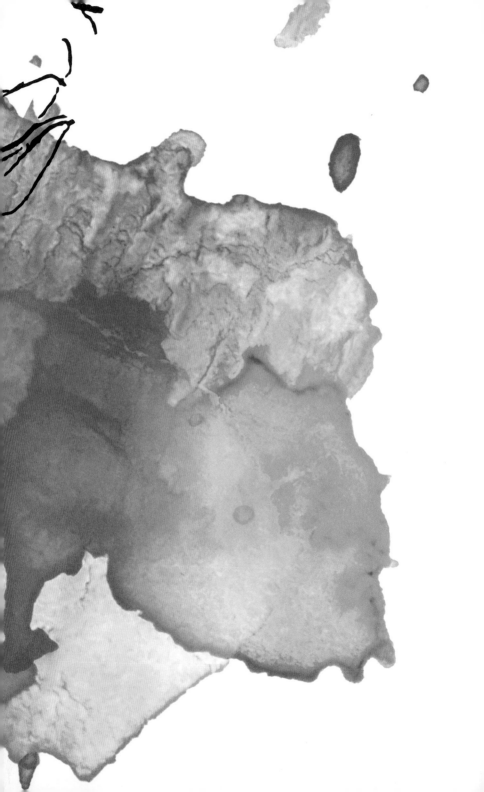

26

The following Monday, Nina and I are sitting in our school's courtyard comparing designs. Instead of going to one of our houses after school, we thought we'd try a new place for inspiration.

"I figured out my casual, lounging around look for Diana Gardo," Nina announces. "Want to see?"

"Sure!" I say.

Nina thrusts her sketch at me. She's obviously excited about it. Once I see it, I completely understand why. The drawing captures Diana's personality perfectly. Nina has sketched her in distressed jeans, silver flats, and a white blazer over a loose T-shirt, then added brown sunglasses and a bright blue scarf as accents.

"I love this," I tell her. "It's stylish and simple, but that pop of color is very you. I know you would have liked to have more."

Nina nods. "That's what the seasonal designs are for," she says. "I chose fall fashions, and I might have gone a little color crazy."

"I bet they look great," I say. "My swimsuit designs are fun, but only the first one is really daring in terms of color." I pull them out of my bag and show her.

"Very pretty," Nina says. "I love the retro theme. The blue and yellow one really stands out. What an awesome idea making a dress out of scuba material."

"Thank you," I say. "That one's my favorite."

"Do you mind taking a look at mine?" Nina asks. "I could use a fresh set of eyes."

"Of course I don't mind," I reply. I flip through her sketchbook until I find the right section. Her first design is a dark blue dress with long sleeves. Nina has styled it with heeled ankle booties and a funky hat.

"I love it," I tell her. "It's so different from your usual style."

Nina beams. "Thanks — it took a lot of self-control not to make it floral. I'm so glad you like it." She turns the page in her sketchbook to a design of a formal dress.

"This is stunning," I say. The dress is a deep purple and embroidered with floral lace design.

"Thank you," says Nina. "I worked hard on that one. I like how it has flowers, but they act as accents."

"Show me more," I say.

"I had trouble with this next one," Nina admits, biting her nail. She holds the sketchpad tightly, not letting me see. "It's supposed to be a work outfit."

"I'm sure it's fine," I say, surprised by her reluctance. In all the years I've known her, I never would have pegged Nina as someone with confidence issues. I guess we all worry about what others think — especially when it comes to something we really care about.

Nina finally loosens her grip, and I look at the sketch. The design — a pink skirt with a cream top and beige pumps — is in the pastel shades Nina tends to prefer. It's as pretty as the others, and I really like the style, but something is a little off.

"I can tell what you're thinking," says Nina. "It's not quite right."

"There's nothing *wrong* with the design," I say. "It just needs something."

"I feel like I need to put more of my own flair into it or something," says Nina, frowning. "It's a little basic as is."

As soon as she says that, something clicks. "That's it! I can really see your personality in your other designs, but less so here, you know?"

"Hmm," says Nina. "Maybe if I added something edgy — like a cool scarf or something? What about something in a darker color like burgundy? Or a tough pattern like a skull print or something?"

"Or maybe a bag," I say. "Something a little edgy in a darker color for contrast."

Nina quickly makes a sketch of the additions. "I'll keep playing with it and see what else I can change. Thanks, Chloe!"

"Any time," I say.

"This has been really helpful," she says. "It's great to have someone to bounce ideas off of. Until you got here, I kept staring at it and thinking it stunk but didn't know why."

"It doesn't stink at all," I insist. "You just needed more of your unique touches."

"I see that now," says Nina. "And I'm glad we can remind each other we don't stink."

I laugh. "It wasn't that long ago that you'd go out of your way to tell me I did."

"Ugh," says Nina, making a face. "I'll never live that down, huh?"

I laugh and shake my head. "Nope. One day we'll be rich and famous, and they'll tell that story on one of those celeb exposés."

"We can only hope," Nina agrees.

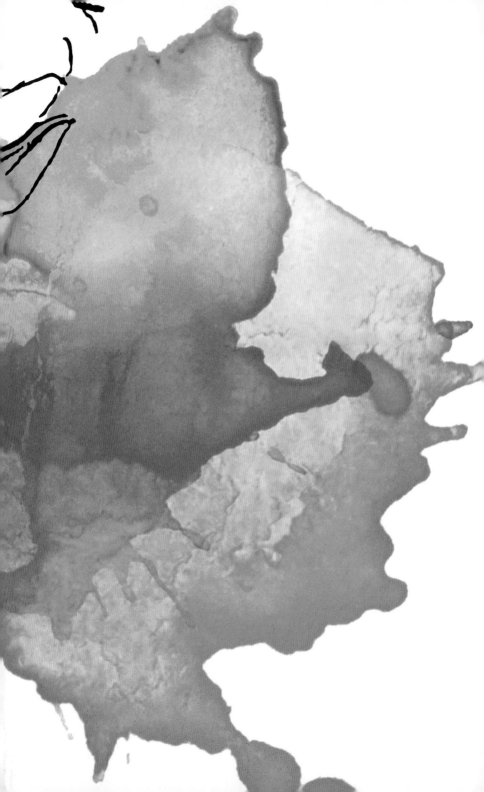

27

Later that week, I'm back in my room with Alex —
except this time I'm packing rather than designing.

Alex holds up a plain white T-shirt. "Are you packing
this too?"

"I guess so?" I say.

Alex laughs and tosses the shirt into my suitcase. "Is
there anything you're *not* packing?"

She has a point. I'm leaving for NYC tomorrow and am
way behind on packing. I should have taken my mom's cue
and started my visual packing list sooner. Since I didn't,
my new strategy is to just throw everything I see into my
suitcase.

"It's too much work," I whine. I tick off the clothes I'll
need on my fingers. "There's the airport outfit, the outfit
I'll wear to dinner tomorrow, my tour outfits —"

"Tour *outfit*," Alex corrects. "Just one. You're going to Parsons and FIT back-to-back. You won't have time to change clothes."

This *should* make things easier, but it doesn't. "Don't I need a back-up outfit? What if I wake up that morning and I'm not in a leggings mood or something?"

"Have some coffee and get in the mood?" suggests Alex. "You won't have any room left in your suitcase at the rate you're going."

I count more fingers. "The hanging out with Bailey on the weekend outfit, the meeting Laura on Monday outfit, and the going back home outfit. That's a lot of clothes!" I stop packing and take out my sketchpad. "I really should make my visual packing list. It will make things easier."

"Good plan," says Alex, holding up a cardigan and T-shirt.

"More clothes?" I ask. "I thought I had to consolidate."

"That was before I remembered that New York in October is probably colder than California in October. You'll want layers."

"Right," I say. I quickly sketch different combinations of sweaters, T-shirts, and blouses. "What do you think of these boots? Brown suede or black?"

"Take them both. You'll use them, and they don't take up that much room," says Alex.

"How about this?" I ask, holding up a gray sweater and pants in one hand and a flowery dress in the other.

"Definitely the sweater," says Alex.

"What about this?" I show her a possible airport look of tan knee-high boots, black leggings, an oversized sweater, and a large scarf.

Alex cocks her head to one side to assess the outfit. "You should add a black bag."

"That's a given," I say. I put the clothes in a maybe pile. I'll decide for sure once I finish my list. "Too bad you can't come with me."

"I know," Alex says, frowning. "It feels like you're never here."

I stop drawing. Alex has made comments like this more and more lately. "That's not really true," I protest.

"Yes," says Alex, "it is." She stares down at the carpet, her face a combination of sadness and annoyance. "This summer you were in New York, two weeks ago you were in LA, and now you're going back to New York. And when you *are* here, you're working on your portfolio or hanging out with Nina."

"Actually," I say, trying to keep my voice calm, "I'm working on my portfolio *with* Nina. It's not like we go out and don't invite you. I do think of her as a friend, but when we're together all we do is work."

"Whatever," Alex mutters.

"I'd love for all of us to hang out together some time. I actually think you guys would get along," I say. "She's not all bad."

Alex throws her hands up in the air. "Now I've heard everything." She rolls her eyes.

I don't know what to say. Alex's jealousy is starting to get old. She's acting like me leaving is only hard on her. It hasn't been easy for me this year, either.

"You're not being fair, Alex," I say.

Suddenly, Alex jumps up. Her eyes are watery, like she's going to start crying. "No," she says, "you're not. Have fun in New York."

"You're leaving?" I say. "But —" My own eyes water, but before I can say anything else, Alex runs downstairs and out of my house, leaving me to finish packing alone.

* * *

The next morning, I'm still thinking about my fight with Alex. I want to text her to apologize, but I don't think I did anything wrong. Besides, she could text me too.

Just forget about it for now, I tell myself. I close my eyes and imagine New York. *That's it. Focus on New York. It will be amazing.*

I put on the airport outfit I decided on (which ends up being a different one than I showed Alex) — an oversized open sweater, gray T-shirt, distressed jeans, and brown suede ankle boots. I pull my hair back in a ponytail and add mirrored sunglasses to hide my sleepy eyes.

"Going incognito?" Mom asks when I get downstairs. She points at the sunglasses.

"I guess I don't need these in the house, huh?" I slip them off. "Do we have coffee?"

Mom pours us both a mug. "We don't have to leave for another hour, so no rush. Are you excited?"

"I am," I say, but I can't get my voice to cooperate.

"You don't sound it," Mom says.

I take a deep breath and tell her about my fight with Alex yesterday. "What should I do? She's my best friend. I don't want to lose her."

"Oh, honey," Mom says, getting up and giving me a hug. "That's the last thing she wants. People handle change in different ways. She's obviously upset about the fact that you might not be near each other next year."

"I am too! Why doesn't she get that?"

"When people are sad, it's sometimes hard for them to see beyond their own feelings. She'll come around." Mom strokes my hair. "I promise."

CHLOE'S
TRAVEL OUTFIT
Sketches

OVERSIZED
SWEATER

STYLISH &
COMFY

DRESSES?

PANTS
OPTIONS

SCARVES &
SWEATERS

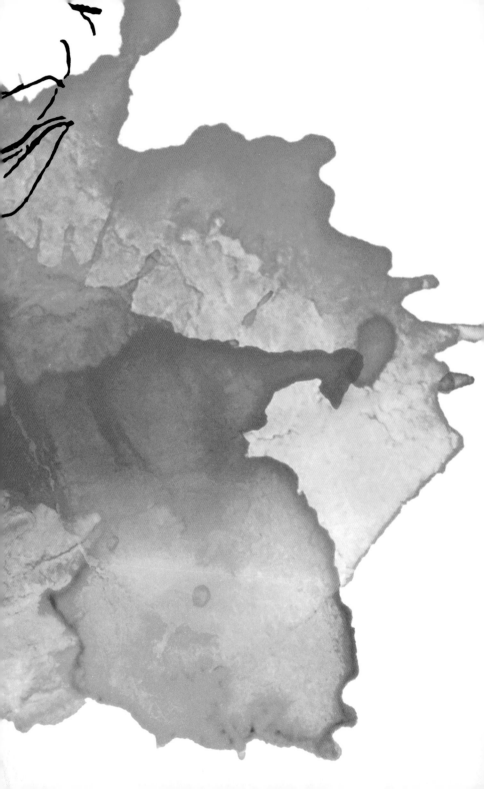

This is going to sound totally crazy, but the moment my mom and I step onto the crowded New York streets, it's as if time stops. It feels like I'm in one of those movies where the character is standing still and the lights, noise, and people zoom around in a blur. Then my mom yells for a taxi, and I'm part of the scene again.

"Doesn't get old, does it?" Mom says as we settle ourselves in the backseat of the taxi.

"What?" I ask, looking out the window.

"New York," Mom says with a smile. "It makes you so happy."

I turn to her. "It really does. After LA, I was a little scared that I wouldn't feel the same about New York. But that's not the case. It just has a different kind of energy."

I gaze out the window as we head to our hotel, taking in all the sights. I've missed this city more than I realized. I'm eager to shower, change, and get ready for a nice dinner. The only bummer is that I'm not sure when I'll see Jake. I asked him about meeting us for dinner tonight, but he wasn't sure he could get free with all his school stuff. The rest of my weekend is filled with tours and other appointments. Why is it that whenever I'm in New York, which is where Jake goes to college, it's so hard to connect with him?

"Why the long face?" Mom asks, noticing my furrowed brow.

"Jake," I say with a sigh. It's no secret that I've been trying to find time to meet up with him.

"Well," Mom says, eyes twinkling, "I'm sure it will work out."

* * *

"You look great!" Mom says as we walk to dinner later that evening. She chose an Italian place with rave online reviews.

"Thanks," I reply. I'm wearing my black suede ankle boots and a long black tunic over black skinny jeans. A white cape coat keeps me warm. I put my hands in my coat pockets and keep my head down to block out the wind.

Alex was right about it being much chillier here than in California. "The menu looked delish, and I'm starving!"

"Here we are!" Mom exclaims a few minutes later. She's been extra chipper since we left the hotel — quite a change from the stressed-out, list-making Mom of last week.

"There you are!" a familiar voice says behind us.

I turn around to see Jake and Liesel standing there! That explains Mom's bubbly attitude. I turn back around to look at her.

"I told you it would work out," Mom says with a wink.

Liesel moves forward to give me a hug. "So great to see you, darling."

I hug her back and then turn to point a mock-accusing finger at Jake. "You!" I say. "You made me think we might not see each other." I'm excited to see him but a little annoyed I thought I might not.

"I wasn't sure if we could make it today," Jake explains, "and I didn't want to disappoint you. Then —"

"Then," my mom interrupts, "when he and Liesel were sure, only a couple days ago, I asked them not to tell you so you'd be surprised."

"I wanted to tell you. Honest," says Jake.

"He really did," my mom agrees. "I'm the one who thought the surprise would be fun. Besides, I didn't want to stress you out about planning *another* outfit."

"Fine," I say with a laugh. "You're all forgiven."

"Phew," Jake says, pretending to wipe sweat from his brow.

We're led to our table, and once we've taken our seats, Liesel turns to me. "So," she says, "I hear you have quite the big day tomorrow."

"More college tours. It's not an easy decision," I say.

"It was simpler for us," says Liesel, motioning to herself and Jake. "I was starting my business in New York, and Jake was already living with me, so he only considered New York schools."

"But even that took time to decide," says Jake.

"What made you choose Parsons over FIT?" I ask. Jake is studying marketing there so he can help with Liesel's ever-expanding business.

Before Jake can answer, the waiter appears to take our order, which is fine, because it seems like Jake is thinking about his answer.

"They're both great schools," says Jake, "but they have different approaches."

"Approaches?"

"Like Parsons is more big picture and creative," he explains. "FIT focuses more on technical stuff, like perfect stitching, things like that. For marketing, Parsons made sense. For designing, I don't know."

"They're both terrific, though," says Liesel. "Truly, Chloe. You can't go wrong."

"We'll see how the tours go, I guess," I say. "But enough about me. Tell me about what's been going on with both of you."

Jake squeezes my hand as Liesel talks about a new fall line she's planning with Stefan. "And Mom convinced Stefan to let me do some behind-the-scenes marketing," he says when she's finished.

"Don't listen to him," says Liesel. "I didn't convince anyone of anything. Jake presented his ideas as part of a class project. They were blind presentations, so Stefan didn't know whose project was whose. He chose Jake without any input from me. Jake never even told me he was applying. I couldn't have helped even if I'd wanted to."

"Lucky break," Jake says, blushing.

My mom looks back and forth between Jake and me, shaking her head. "No wonder you get along so well. Neither of you give yourself enough credit."

Our food arrives just then, and Liesel and my mom talk about getting together tomorrow while I'm at Bailey's dorm. Meanwhile Jake and I have our own quiet conversation.

"I missed you," he says. "I know it wasn't that long ago that I was in California, but still. I wish you were staying longer."

"Me too," I say. "These next few days are so packed."

"But," Jake says, lacing his fingers with mine, "in just a couple weeks I'll be back in Santa Cruz for your Winter Formal. Save me a dance?"

"Just one?" I joke. "I was planning to save you so many."

Jake blushes. "I was hoping you'd say that." He pauses for a second, looking serious. "Promise me something."

"What?" I ask.

"Have fun tomorrow. Don't worry about which college you're going to end up at. You're in New York, you're going to see Bailey, and you get to visit two great schools. There will be plenty of time to worry about making a decision later. Just give yourself a break and enjoy the tours and city."

Jake is so right. I'd like to do that, even if *not* worrying isn't exactly me. I squeeze his hand. "I'll try."

241

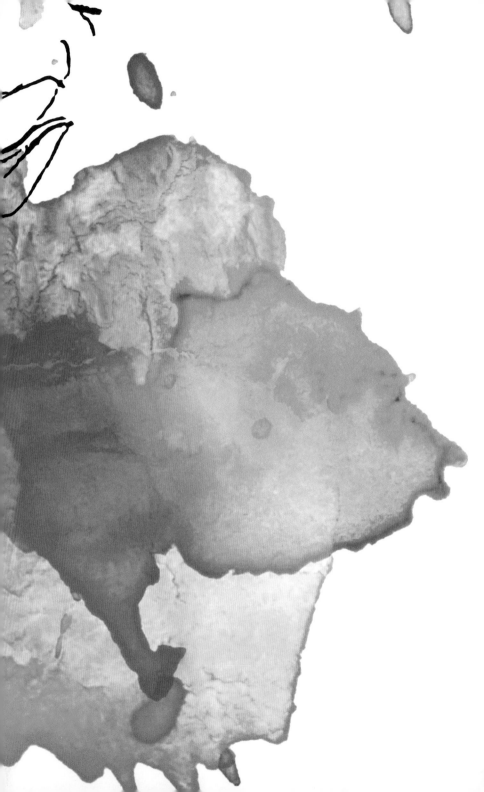

29

"Here we go," I say as my mom and I walk into FIT for our tour Saturday morning. I'm excited and trying to follow Jake's advice.

"You fit right in," Mom says, admiring my outfit.

"I do my best," I reply. Today, I picked a black off-the-shoulder top and paired it with dark jeans and a green bag.

In the entry area, there's a group already waiting. A tall girl wearing an oversized black sweater layered over a gray T-shirt, black leggings, and silver flats greets us.

"Hi, everyone!" she says. "I'm Whitney, and I'll be your guide today."

"That looks like something you'd wear," Mom whispers.

"That's a good sign," I whisper back.

"There are so many great things about FIT," Whitney continues, "but one of my favorites is the location. We're so

close to the Garment District, which means you'll really get a feel for the city and fashion industry here. At FIT, we say, 'NYC is your campus.'"

I can't help but smile at that. There are so many amazing resources here.

Whitney looks at a piece of paper in her hand. "I see you're all interested in the School of Art and Design, so let's start there." She leads us to a large, brown building. Unlike FIDM, the walls here are not brightly colored. Instead, they're plain and wooden. It's a bit of a letdown.

I follow Whitney into a classroom and notice framed pictures of student designs on the walls. That's a really nice touch. Who wouldn't be motivated by seeing other students' designs on display? It makes me think of Nina and how useful reviewing our designs together has been.

All around the room, students have their own mannequins and are concentrating on measuring fabric. The professor is explaining something about precise stitching. The tips he gives are impressive, and he describes them in great detail.

"They're pretty no-nonsense here when it comes to learning," says Whitney. "I considered myself a good designer when I entered this program, but I realized I still had so much to learn. If you want to get better with your technique, this is the school for you."

I think about what I've accomplished so far and the dresses I've designed for the upcoming Winter Formal. Then I imagine myself in these seats, ready to be made better.

"You'll also learn about professional patternmaking, sewing techniques, and draping, as well as how to make designs on the computer," Whitney continues.

When I was doing my internship at Stefan Meyers, I did all my designs by hand, but I noticed several designers who did them only on computer. I don't know how to do computer design, but I should.

"Let me take you to my favorite spot — the Museum at FIT," Whitney says, leading us out of the classroom. "They have fabulous exhibitions and programs. I love going there for inspiration."

When we arrive at the museum, I can see why. The current exhibition is of 1930s fashion. There's a gown in ivory tulle and gold threading that cascades to the floor. I love its glamour. My mom points out an orange swimsuit with black and gold geometric patterns.

"It's wool!" says Mom. "Odd choice for a bathing suit."

"It wouldn't be my first choice, either," I say with a laugh.

We walk around the museum, and I pay extra attention to the dresses. I compare them to my designs and think about what I might do differently. I imagine myself coming here to unwind, sketchpad in hand. I take it out now and do a quick sketch of a favorite piece. It's a gown in ivory silk organza with black lace insets. There's a teardrop opening in the back. I put a little star by it to remind myself to incorporate it into my designs.

Whitney talks more about campus life and what the school can offer. "There are pros and cons to all fashion schools," she tells us. "Not only is FIT affordable — about a third of what Parsons costs — but you'll leave college prepared for a career in fashion."

I see parents and students perk up at the mention of the tuition cost. My mom stands straighter too. I know she said we could handle a more expensive school if I got a job, but a good education at a fraction of the cost is definitely something to consider.

"We also have an annual student runway show that top designers critique," says Whitney. "And you'll have the opportunity to intern with excellent designers. You can even study in Milan for a semester."

"Milan!" I whisper to my mom, and she smiles.

"In the end," says Whitney, "you have to try and imagine where you see yourself and decide which school is the best fit for you."

That's the plan, I think to myself. One school left.

TEARDROP OPENING

BLACK LACE INSETS

FIT MUSEUM *Designs*

IVORY SILK ORGANZA

DOODLES AND *Ideas*

College **CHLOE**

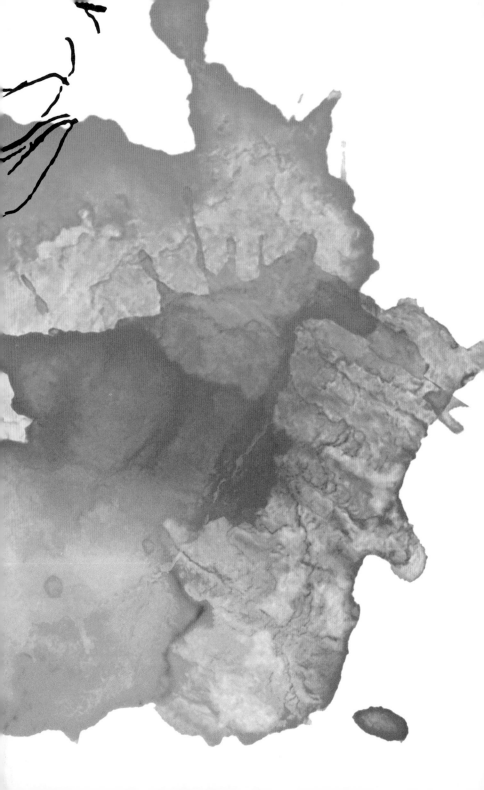

"Wow!" I say as our Parsons tour guide, Sammi, leads us into the hallway of the fashion campus later that afternoon. The day has been jam-packed — Mom and I hurried here straight from FIT — but I still have time to be impressed. The walls here are lined with framed illustrations of vintage clothing, all of which are beautiful.

I stare at a display labeled *Wedding Dresses* — although the designs look more like spring or summer party dresses. They're all done in white and have cinched waists, but their details set them apart. One has a ruffled lace skirt. Another has a black ribbon decorating the bodice. A third dress has a blue sash.

251

It's amazing how the smallest details can completely change the look of a piece. I think of my portfolio too. From the swimsuits to my Winter Formal dresses, I've played with embellishments and details to create something unique each time. Until this moment, though, I sort of thought of my portfolio as something I was working on for the end goal — to get into college. These designs make me realize it's so much more. My portfolio is proof of how much I've learned and how far I've come as a designer.

Sammi leads us into a classroom. For once, there isn't a class going on. This allows me to really inspect the room without worrying that I'll be in someone's way.

"Our classrooms are a little sparse," Sammi says, "but having fewer distractions always helps me focus. And the windows are one of my favorite parts."

She points to the wide, tall windows that overlook 7th Avenue, and I imagine sitting and sketching by one of those or just staring out as I put the finishing touches on a design.

"The mirrors and sewing machines are another highlight." Sammi waves her arm, motioning around the space. The walls are lined with fitting mirrors — a great touch for when you're trying to see exactly how a garment looks. There are also sewing machines across the wall.

I think back to my time on *Teen Design Diva* — getting a sewing machine was a scramble, and before that we had to hand-sew our garments. I would have killed for a room like this.

As the group heads out of the classroom, a girl in a black blazer, studded T-shirt, torn jeans, and wedge sneakers speaks up. "So are all the classes in this building?"

Sammi laughs. "I wish! They're spread out across eight streets. That's something you're going to have to budget for. Always leave extra time."

"At FIT, all the classes are on one street," I say to my mom.

"Pros and cons list, right?" says my mom.

"That's a good idea," I agree. "As of now, they're not all that different."

"Do you have a museum?" the girl in the blazer asks.

"We don't," says Sammi. "But we do have our annual Fashion Benefit and Parsons Festival. The benefit highlights the work of graduating students and raises money for scholarships. Top designers who've graduated from Parsons attend it. It's really exciting!"

I remember FIT and FIDM discussing something similar. I love that each has its own opportunity to showcase designs.

"The festival has all kinds of events and exhibitions," Sammi explains. "And it showcases student work from all of Parsons's programs."

"Do you have an exhibition now?" another girl on the tour asks. She's wearing a leopard-print blazer over jeans and the ends of her hair are dyed purple.

"We do! Thanks for the reminder. Follow me." Sammi leads us into a room with student designs. The current theme appears to be feathers. The showcased dresses all use them in some way. A red dress stands out the most. The bodice is red satin and resembles a corset, and the skirt is asymmetrical and comprised of feathers.

The girl in the leopard-print blazer raises her hand again. "This is all very cool, and Parsons seems like a great school, but I've toured a few fashion schools already. Can't you just tell me why Parsons is the best choice?"

Sammi forces a smile. "Well, we have a great faculty. Our students leave very prepared and have real designers as mentors. Our exhibitions are great opportunities —"

"Everyone says that," the girl interrupts, rolling her eyes.

Sammi looks flustered for a moment but then says, "I love it here. My classmates are all really talented, and I love how my teachers encourage creativity. But I can't tell you what school to pick. It comes down to what's right for you."

What *is* right for me? That seems to be the million-dollar question. Too bad I don't have an answer.

ELEGANT

FIT
TOUR
Designs

SATIN
FABRIC

CORSET
BODICE

ASYMMETRICAL!

RUFFLES

FEATHERED
SKIRT

· Student Designs
· Feath

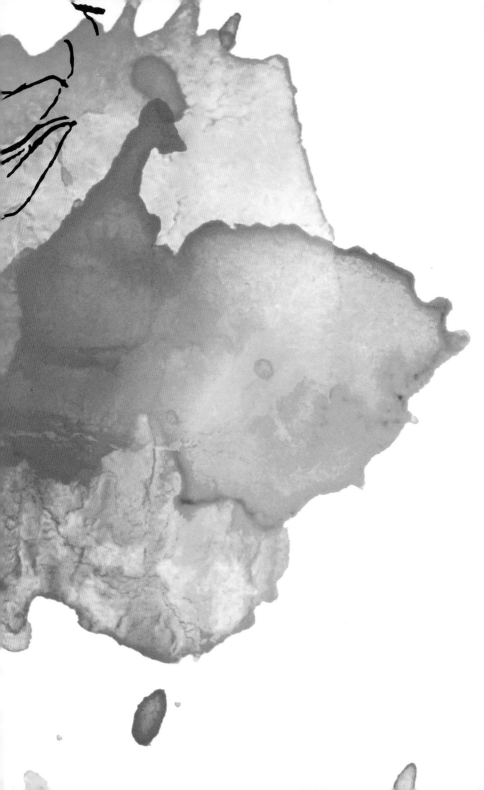

31

"Chloe!" Bailey, my former suitemate, exclaims. She grins as she holds open the door to her dorm later that evening. "You're looking as stylish as ever!"

"You too!" I say. My one-time roommate looks adorable in a white cropped sweater and matching skirt paired with floral-print shoes.

Bailey pulls me into the room and tosses her phone to a redhead in the room. "Ellen, can you take a picture of us?" Without waiting for a response, she puts her hand on her hip and strikes a pose.

I laugh and pose alongside her. "So what's on the agenda for tonight?" I ask once Ellen has snapped our picture.

Ellen hands Bailey's phone back and bounces on her toes. "There's a great dance club and restaurant that just

BAILEY &
ROOMMATE
Designs

INFINITY
SCARF

CROPPED
SWEATER

BLACK SHIRT
& RED
CARDIGAN

PEARL
BUTTONS

FLORAL-
PRINT
SHOES

MINISKIRT

LEGGINGS
& LACE-UP
BOOTS

opened nearby. We've been dying to check it out because we it have on good authority —"

Bailey laughs. "I'd hardly call a gossip magazine good authority."

"As I was saying," Ellen continues, face serious, "we have it on good authority that there have been several celebrity sightings there."

"Did someone say celebrity?" asks a girl standing just outside Bailey's open door. Her style — a red sweater over a black shirt with pearl buttons, black leggings, and lace-up brown boots — is very similar to my own. The white scarf wrapped around her neck brightens the ensemble.

"Hey, Andrea. Come on in! Meet Chloe."

"Oh my gosh," Andrea says, her eyes growing wide. "Chloe Montgomery? I loved you on *Teen Design Diva!*"

My face reddens. "Thanks. It's nice to meet you."

"Bailey, why didn't you tell me she'd be here today?" Andrea demands.

Bailey and Ellen exchange eye rolls. "Uh, *this* is why, Miss Fangirl," Bailey says.

Over the next few minutes, more people pop into Bailey and Ellen's room to offer quick hellos. It's so busy. Living here in the summer wasn't the same. We weren't in our room very much. And when we were, our door was closed.

"Is it always like this?" I ask.

Ellen, Andrea, and Bailey look confused. "What do you mean?" Bailey asks.

"Like people popping in, your door open, everyone being so friendly," I say.

"Oh!" says Bailey. "I'm so used to it, I don't even notice anymore. But, yeah, that's the best part about living in a dorm. You're never alone — unless you want to be."

"Is it weird for you?" asks Ellen. "We can close the door."

"No!" I say. "It's actually really cool. Are the dorms at all colleges like this?" I'm sort of hoping they'll say no — then I can add this to my pro list for FIT.

"Yup!" says Andrea. "I've visited friends at Parsons and other colleges outside the city too. It's the same everywhere."

"Oh," I say, my face falling.

Bailey looks confused. "You just said it was cool."

"It *is*," I say, "but I'm trying to decide on a school, and they're all pretty similar."

Ellen gives me a knowing look. "I remember going through that. It's really hard to know which one is right for you. But you'll figure it out."

Bailey checks her watch. "Let's get out of here. Chloe needs some new scenery."

* * *

The restaurant we go to is called Plush. I'm assuming it gets its name from the soft, burgundy cushions surrounding each dimly lit sitting area. "Fancy," I say when we get to our table.

"Wow," says Andrea. "Isn't that Kylie King, the lead of *Silvertown*? And, whoa. Is that Harvey Kahn? And, wait . . ." Andrea goes on to list five other celebs, eyes getting bigger and bigger with each one.

Ellen and Bailey glance around the restaurant as Andrea points everyone out. They're not as giddy as she is, but I am. I think about how excited Alex would be to be here. We still haven't talked since our fight. I texted her after we landed, and she hasn't written back.

"Ladies," a waiter says, approaching our table. "Here are your appetizers."

I dig in. "When did we order these?" I ask in between bites.

"You learn things here," says Bailey, putting an arm around me. "We called them in before we came."

"Yep," says Ellen, "stick with us and college will be a breeze."

I get a warm, happy feeling. Going to college in New York *would* be great. I'd have a built-in friend network, not to mention Jake and Liesel would be nearby. And living so close to the Fashion District and museums is what I've always wanted. But on the other hand, FIDM would be close to Alex's college and my family. Plus, the beauty of FIDM with its colorful walls, floor, and unique students is still on my brain.

"It's definitely appealing," I finally say.

"Hold up," Ellen says, staring across the room. "No way."

I follow her gaze. "Oh my god. No way," I repeat.

"That's Lola James!" Andrea practically squeals.

"I drew her!" I blurt out. "She's my portfolio inspiration!" The girls look at me, confused. "The portfolio requirements for FIT — I have to draw pop star designs," I babble. "Never mind! Just wow."

For once, I don't have my sketchpad with me. Even if I did, I doubt I'd have the guts to approach Lola, so I settle for staring. Despite it being October, Lola is dressed in a black velvet top, a gold skirt with an embroidered leaf design, and black heels. I think about the designs I created for her. They're different, but I think they truly capture her style, too.

"You should tell her she inspired you," Bailey teases, pretending to push me from our table toward Lola.

"Do it!" Andrea says. "You're famous, too." Unlike Bailey, she seems serious.

"Um, I don't think so. We're in a different league of famous," I say.

"Still," Ellen says, "what can it hurt?"

I shake my head. "Sorry. That's just not me."

"It may not be you," Bailey says, looking back across the room, "but it's definitely Lola. She's walking over here."

We all look toward the empty appetizer plate on our table and try to keep cool.

"Hi," says Lola. She's even more beautiful in person. "This is going to sound incredibly dorky, but I'm a huge fan of you and *Teen Design Diva*. I'm Lola James."

I laugh nervously. "Um, I know who you are. *Everyone* knows who you are. I'm Chloe Montgomery."

Duh, Chloe, I think. Obviously she knows that — she introduced herself to *me*.

"Chloe drew designs for you," Andrea suddenly blurts out. I elbow her hard in the side.

Lola's eyebrows go up. "Really?"

"Well, um, it was for a college admission thing," I mumble.

Lola smiles. "Cool. I'd love to see them sometime. Maybe I'll wear something of yours one day."

"No," I try to explain, "they're not actually . . ." I stop talking. Lola looks like she's ready to go back to her table. "It was great meeting you."

"Same! I'll keep my eye out for your stuff," Lola says, walking away with a wave.

"She'll keep an eye out!" says Ellen.

"For your stuff!" says Bailey.

"Didn't I say you were famous?" Andrea shrieks.

I blush. I can't wait to tell Alex about my encounter. She might not be ready to talk yet, but I text her anyway: *OMG! I just ran into Lola James at a restaurant here — she said she'd want to wear my designs!*

I spend the rest of the night talking and laughing with Bailey and her friends, but I can't keep from checking my phone. But as fun as it is, I can't ignore how hurt I am by Alex's silence.

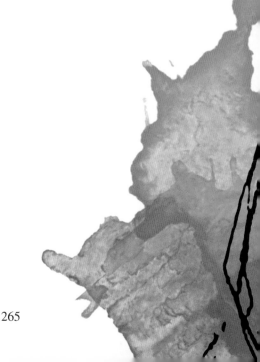

On Monday morning, I get a text from Laura asking to postpone our meeting by an hour because things are crazy busy at Stefan Meyers. I smile when I see the message. Things were always insanely busy during my internship — nothing has changed apparently.

"Just remember we have to catch our flight home later this afternoon," Mom reminds me as I model another outfit in front of her hotel room mirror.

I do a twirl to view the outfit from all angles. Yep, these black leather leggings, black boots, and gray sweater over a collared shirt are definitely the winner. "I remember."

I'm excited to see Laura today, but I can't stop thinking about the total silence from Alex. She's supposed to be my best friend. I get that she might be upset about the

CHLOE'S
NYC OUTFIT
Design

PONYTAIL
&
SCARF

GRAY
SWEATER

WHITE
BUTTON-
DOWN
SHIRT

LEATHER
LEGGINGS

TALL BLACK
BOOTS

possibility of me going to school in New York and maybe she feels left out, but her ignoring me is not okay. When I get home, we're going to have a heart-to-heart and work this out once and for all.

* * *

When I arrive at Stefan Meyers, Laura is waiting for me in the lobby. "Chloe!" she exclaims, hurrying over and giving me a hug. "It's so good to see you! Come on upstairs with me, and I'll show you what we've been up to."

I follow Laura to the elevator. When the doors open on her floor, I see interns and designers hard at work sketching on computers, creating vision boards, and sorting through samples.

Laura leads me to her office, which is surprisingly organized — especially for her. "Check out these designs," she says, showing me sketches of minidresses that look like they were inspired by the 1960s. "We're thinking bright and bold."

"They're so fun!" I say, looking at a long-sleeved, above-the-knee dress with big, multicolored strokes in yellow, red, green, and orange.

"It's definitely a change from the art deco line you worked on this summer, but I love getting the chance to explore different design elements," Laura says.

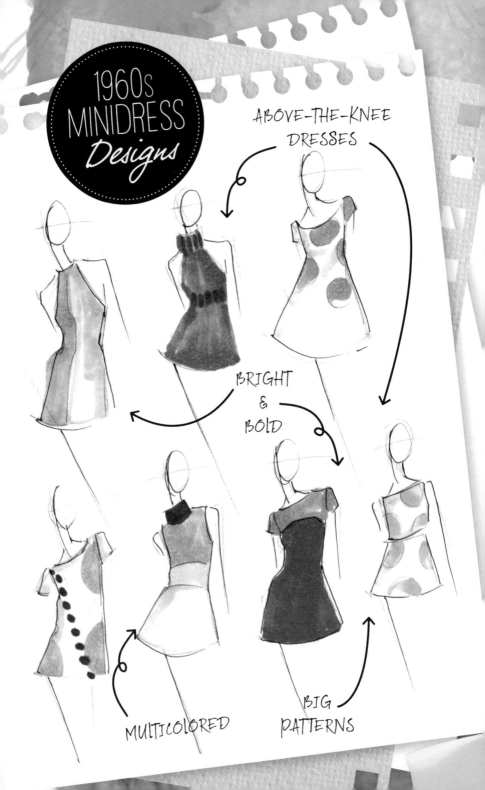

"Me too!" I agree. "In fact, that's exactly what I'm trying to do with my portfolio for college applications." I pull out my portfolio, which I brought with me, and briefly tell Laura about the range I'm trying to show.

Laura gives a low whistle. "That's a lot of work," she says, flipping through my sketches, "but I'm really proud of you. I can definitely see the growth in your designs. I especially love these bathing suit transformations."

"Thank you," I say.

"That reminds me," says Laura, "Stefan wanted to meet with you, but he had a meeting. He asked me to find out about your plans for next summer. I know it's incredibly far in advance, but we were hoping you might be willing to intern again next year."

"Willing? I'm definitely willing!" Regardless of my college plans, I can spend a summer in New York. "Thank you!"

"Excellent," says Laura. "We'll discuss more this spring. In the meantime, how is your college search going?"

I sigh. "It's going. But I don't know how I'm ever going to make a decision. I've toured FIDM, FIT, and Parsons, and they all seem great. I know it sounds so dramatic, but it feels like if I choose wrong, I could totally mess up my future."

Laura pats my hand sympathetically. "I know it seems like that, and I'm not saying choosing the right college isn't important, but there are a lot of paths to the same end goal. Did you know I went to college for math? I thought I was going to do something with finance or numbers."

My jaw drops. "Really?"

Laura nods. "Yup. I was really good at it. I still am. But designing was my first love. I had twenty notebooks full of sketches. I made a ton of my own clothes. I was a lot like you."

"No wonder we get along," I say with a laugh.

Laura smiles. "I didn't think I could make a career out of fashion design. I knew people did, but I thought I needed something more stable. Long story short, I got my math degree. Worked in a high-profile company for a while. Spent more time doodling dresses and shoes than I did doodling dollar signs and finally went back to school for a fashion degree. I would have liked to pursue my dream sooner, but it is what it is. At least I'm here."

"Wow," I say. "That's pretty impressive."

"And I'll tell you another secret — Taylor went to Parsons, Stefan went to FIT, and Michael went to FIDM," she says, listing off my other internship supervisors on her fingers.

"And they're all here," I say.

"Exactly," says Laura. "Your dream is to have your own label. I suspect that no matter where you go to school, you'll get there. You have drive. You'll do great anywhere."

I smile. Her confidence in me means so much. "Thanks."

Laura looks at the clock on her wall. "Well, kid, you have a plane to catch, and I'm up to my eyeballs in work — as always." She chuckles. "But it was so great to see you. I'll be in touch. And think about what I said, okay?"

"I will," I say, giving her a hug goodbye. "It was great seeing you!"

As I head back to the elevator, I take a lingering look around the design room and think about how only three months ago I was in the same spot. Everything feels like it's moving so quickly lately.

Outside, I spot a girl, probably about my age, standing at the curb. She's holding a suitcase with one arm and waving for a taxi with the large, gray purse that's in her other hand. It's cloudy, but she's wearing black oversized sunglasses anyway. A loose gray sweater hangs over her fitted blue jeans.

As I watch, the girl steps to the side to avoid putting her red suede ankle boots in a puddle and adjusts the long gold chain around her neck. A taxi finally pulls up, and the girl shoves her suitcase into the trunk before settling in the backseat.

I wonder where she goes to school and if she's on her way to the airport to visit her family. Like I'll be doing next year — wherever I end up.

Just then my phone buzzes with a text from my mom, and I head back to the hotel. There are still things to figure out — my portfolio, last-minute Winter Formal dresses, Alex's dress, and Alex herself. But I keep Laura's words at the forefront of my mind. In time, I'll find my path, and I'll get there.

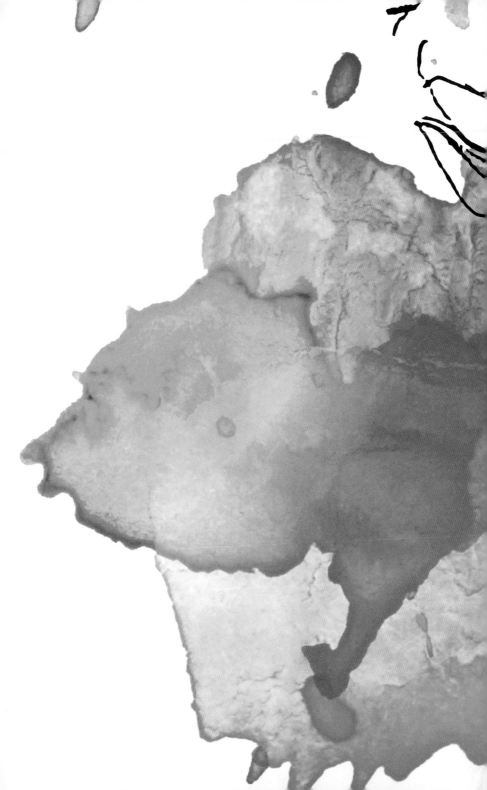

Dear Diary,

Not to sound completely cheesy, but where has my life gone?! It seems like just yesterday that I was sitting in my living room, dreaming of winning *Teen Design Diva*, and now here I am applying for college! It feels like everything is finally coming together on that front. Believe it or not, I'm on track with my applications; I should have my portfolio requirements done in the next few weeks. And I finally finished my college tours.

I'd be lying if I said I'm not stressing at all, but I am much calmer than I was at the start of the school year. (I guess it would be hard not to be, though, right?) Seeing Jake and Liesel in New York was fantastic, and talking with Laura helped a lot. She made me realize that there's more than one path to my dream of being a designer. I'll get there no matter which college I end up at. Besides, I need to prioritize my worries. Freaking out over which college to go to when my applications aren't even complete isn't logical. I have two more immediate problems:

1. I still need to finish the last of my Winter Formal designs — a dress for me, a dress for Alex, and a

dress for one final client. Thank goodness Mimi planned ahead and factored in extra time for those designs.

2. I have to deal with my BFF, who's being a little irrational.

I just don't get why Alex is giving me the cold shoulder. My mom says when people are sad about something they deal with it in different ways. That's the only reason I can think of for Alex picking fights with me and acting so distant. I know she's upset about me touring NYC schools and forming a friendship with Nina, but now she's not even returning my texts.

I know she told me to surprise her with her dress design, but not having Alex in my life makes working on her dress way less fun in general. I only hope we can work things out! Senior year without my best friend by my side is *not* what I had in mind.

Xoxo — Chloe

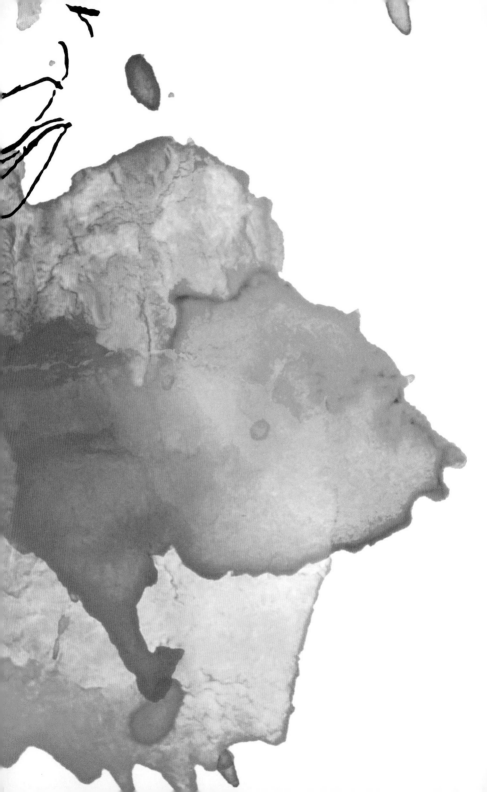

33

"Hey," Alex says, sitting beside me in the courtyard during lunch on Thursday.

It's been two days since I've been back from New York, and most of our conversations have consisted of single-syllable words. I'm actually surprised she's eating with me today at all.

"Hey," I reply. "Cute outfit."

Alex smooths her polka-dot peplum top and adjusts her black leggings. "Thanks." She takes a bite of her turkey sandwich, then says, "I like your romper too."

The romper is all black, but the gold collar adds flair. "Thanks," I say, sticking with our single-syllable trend.

ALEX'S SCHOOL OUTFIT *Design*

CM

BLACK & WHITE COLOR PALETTE

SLEEVELESS BLOUSE

PEPLUM HEMLINE

POLKA DOTS

BLACK LEGGINGS

BLACK HIGH HEELS

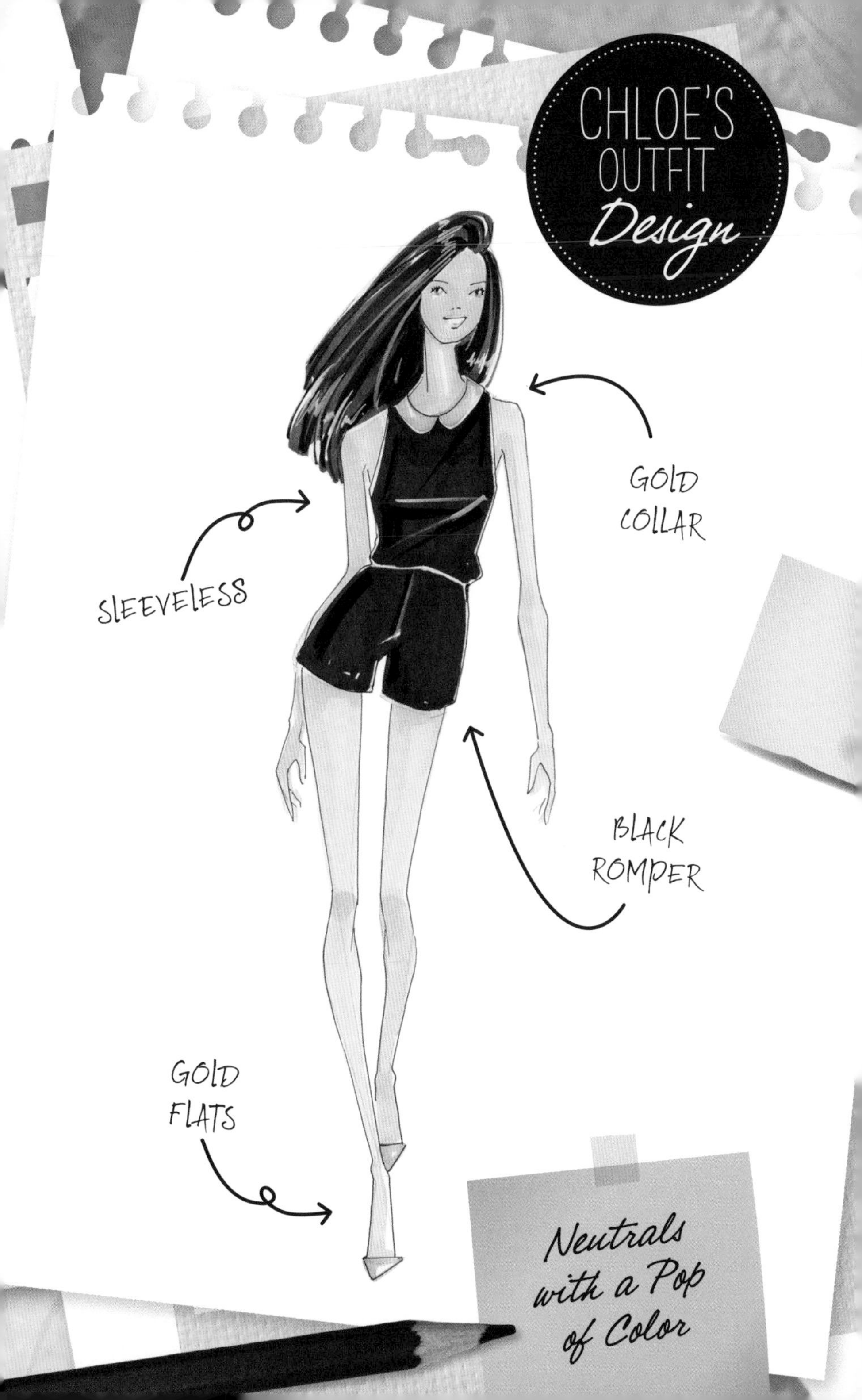

CHLOE'S OUTFIT
Design

GOLD
COLLAR

SLEEVELESS

BLACK
ROMPER

GOLD
FLATS

Neutrals
with a Pop
of Color

When Alex doesn't say anything else, I look down and focus on eating my yogurt. I'm hurt she never answered my texts from New York. She never even said anything about me meeting Lola James. I would have thought a celebrity run-in — with a famous pop star, no less — would be more than enough to break the ice. The more I think about all that, the angrier I get.

"Look —" I begin just as Alex says, "Chloe —"

Normally, this kind of thing would make us laugh, but not today.

"You can go first," I say.

Alex takes a deep breath. "I'm sorry. I know I've been acting badly. I don't know what's wrong with me. I'm really happy for you, but I feel left out."

"I understand that," I say. "I felt left out when I came back at the end of the summer, remember? You had new friends and a new boyfriend. But that didn't make me ignore you."

Alex hangs her head. "I know."

I stir the fruit in my yogurt, trying to blend it perfectly. I've never fought with Alex like this before, and it feels completely awful. I want to get past this, but the ball is in her court.

"I didn't answer your texts while you were in New York because I was embarrassed about how I acted before you left," Alex says. "I know I was being dumb about you being friends with Nina. I didn't know what to say." Her voice wobbles, like she's going to cry.

I take a break from mixing the yogurt to look at her. I can tell she's trying to make things right.

"Do you want to hear about it now?" I ask.

Alex's eyes light up. "Definitely! Tell me every detail about meeting Lola James. What did you wear? What did she say? What did you eat?"

I laugh. "What did I eat? Is that really exciting to you?"

Alex opens her snack bag of Doritos. "Obviously," she says. "I'm trying to visualize the situation. Food helps set the mood."

I laugh again and tell her all about the restaurant — including everything I ordered — and my outfit. When I start to explain how I debated going up to Lola, Alex interrupts.

"Wait, wait, wait." Her mouth drops open in surprise. "You went up to *her*? I don't think even I could have done that."

I smile. "You interrupted before I could finish. I *thought* about going up to her. *She* came to *me*. I don't think I could have actually approached her, either. I was *way* too nervous."

"Ugh, I wish I'd been there," says Alex. "What happened next? You texted me something about her wanting to wear your designs?"

"Yep," I say, nodding. "Bailey and her college friends talked me up, and the next thing I knew, I was daydreaming about Lola wearing my stuff on the red carpet."

Alex's face grows serious. "She will one day, you know. Your designs are amazing."

"Thanks," I say. For the first time in a week, the one-word answer doesn't feel curt. It finally feels like things are getting back to normal. Like Alex and I can be friends like we used to.

"If you end up in New York, promise that we'll find Lola when I visit," Alex says. "Even if we have to go to every restaurant in the city."

"Of course!" I say. "We won't sleep until you get to shake Lola's hand."

"Perfect," Alex says with a smile.

"Now that we're back on speaking terms, there's actually something else I've been wanting to talk to you about," I tell her. "And it's important — your dress for Winter Formal."

Alex puts her fingers in her ears and starts humming to drown me out. "I don't want to know. I want it to be a surprise."

I roll my eyes and push her hands down away from her ears. "Fine, but don't blame me if you end up with a dress you hate."

Alex shakes her head. "That won't happen," she insists. "There's no way I could hate any of your designs. But maybe we could go shopping after school today. You know, for inspiration."

My face gets hot, and I look down, avoiding her gaze. "I can't today."

Alex makes a face. "Portfolio stuff to work on?" she guesses.

"Sort of . . ." I say vaguely. I do have to work on my portfolio, but I'm worried that if I tell Alex who I'm working with it will start another fight. I don't want to lie to her, but I can't deal with anymore drama. "I wish I could go," I add, which is totally true.

"Chloe!" says a voice behind us. "I've been looking for you everywhere!"

Alex tenses as Nina walks toward us. She's smiling, but Alex isn't.

"Hey, Nina," I say.

"Hey," she replies. "Just wanted to make sure we're still on for after school."

Alex sets her lips in a tight line and glares at me. "I see how it is," she says.

"Alex, we're working on our portfolios together," I say, feeling exasperated. I thought we just solved this issue, and now . . .

"Whatever," Alex mutters. She gets to her feet, grabs her bag, and storms off.

Nina looks confused. "Did I do something wrong? Was I not supposed to say anything?"

I shake my head. "It's not you. Don't worry about it. Alex and I have been having issues, but I think I know how to make things better."

Nina raises an eyebrow. "Oh, yeah?"

I nod. "Yep. But I'll need your help."

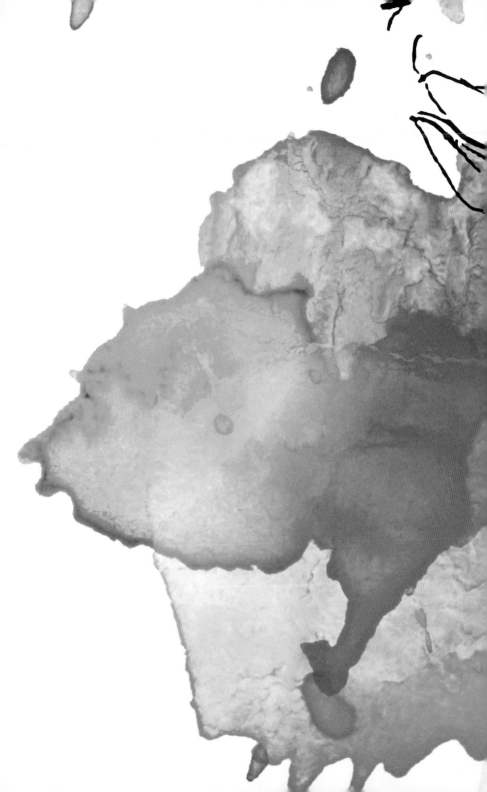

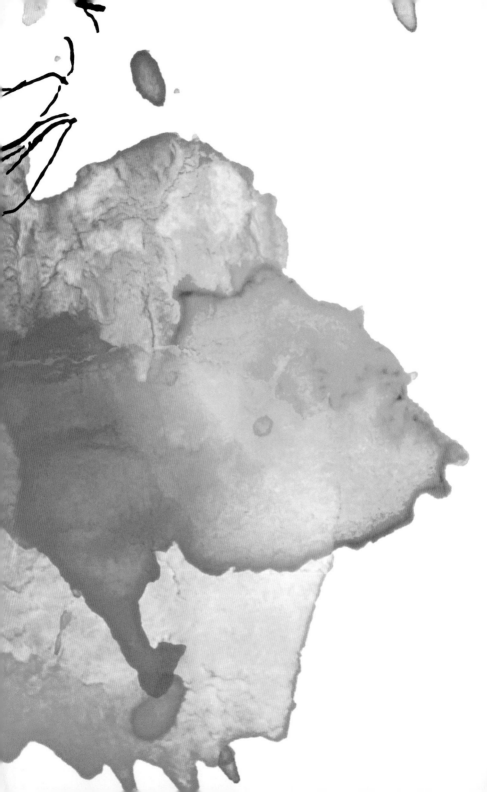

34

"Are you kidding me?" Nina asks when I tell her about my plan. "You want *me* to help you with Alex's dress?"

"I know you guys don't get along that well, but —"

"'Don't get along' is putting it nicely," Nina interrupts. "She hates me!"

"She doesn't *hate* you," I say. "And, anyway, it's not really about *you*."

Nina frowns. "It sure *feels* like it's about me when she ignores me or makes snide comments."

"You're not perfect, either," I mumble.

"Um, that doesn't sound like someone who needs my help," Nina says.

"Hear me out," I say. "Please?"

Nina sucks in air through her teeth and closes her eyes. "Fine," she says, slowly opening her eyes and letting out a slow, even breath. "Explain."

"Alex is upset about things changing. She's sad I might be leaving California. And she feels left out. She's more into fashion than she used to be, but it's still not her passion."

Nina's face softens. "I get all that, but that doesn't change the fact that she has this thing against me."

"Like I said, I don't think it's about you. I think seeing us connect over something she's not a part of makes her feel like she doesn't fit in with me."

"But that's silly!" says Nina. "There's more to life than fashion. You two have lots of other things in common."

"I know," I say, "but I think she's too upset to see this right now. Plus, it's not like you've gone out of your way to connect with *her*."

"Yeah, yeah," Nina mutters.

"I have a few ideas for her dress, but I keep second-guessing myself. It has to be perfect. And I think a fresh perspective would help. You can help me narrow down ideas and brainstorm. *And*," I add when I see Nina open her mouth to interrupt, "it will show her you're not the enemy. You guys really aren't all that different, but neither of you wants to see that. This will help."

Nina sighs and flips through her sketchbook. Just as I begin to wonder if she's stopped considering my idea and moved on to something else, she says, "I *do* need more Winter Formal dress designs for my portfolio."

I grin. "There you go! Win-win for all!"

"Show me what you've got so far," says Nina somewhat grudgingly.

"I *love* your enthusiasm," I say sarcastically, causing Nina to roll her eyes. I open my sketchpad to show samples of tops and bottoms. "I'm thinking of some kind of sporty-inspired look."

"That makes sense for Alex. I think she'd like that."

"What do you think of a fitted jersey-style top and flowy skirt but in silk?" I point to a design I was working on yesterday of a baseball-tee inspired gown in black and white.

Nina leans in to get a better look. "It's very pretty — and no frills, which I think Alex would like. But I could also see her going a little edgier. She's stepped up her style game this past year."

I nod. "I feel the same way. I played around with the same design in brighter colors, but that still doesn't feel like enough."

"The colors do add something," says Nina, "but, yeah, you need more."

"I was kind of hoping it was just me being hard on myself, and you'd tell me it was perfect, and I'd be done," I say with a laugh.

"I'm not saying they're not good," Nina says. "Just not quite right for Alex's Winter Formal dress. You said you wanted *perfect*."

I sigh. "You're right. What about these?" I show her a page of fancier tops incorporating sporty looks. There's one that has tank top features, another with sporty stripes, and a third that looks like a mesh jersey. I also played with zipper designs, neon colors, and reflective tape.

"These are all very cool," says Nina. "I like the idea of a fitted top with a flowing skirt. Maybe in lilac?"

"Lilac, huh?" I say. "And flowing skirt? That *would* look awesome. On *you*."

Nina blushes. "Sorry. You're right — not exactly Alex's style." She makes a note in her sketchpad so she won't forget her idea. "But back to Alex."

Suddenly, she jumps up. "Wait! That first design made me think of something. The fitted top reminds me of one of those sporty swimsuits you have in your portfolio for FIDM. What if you do something like that scuba dress you designed for that? The material is definitely sporty."

I turn the pages of my sketchbook to those designs. Nina is right; that dress is definitely edgy, sporty, and unique. If I just change the colors and tweak the fabric . . . yes! That would look amazing on Alex.

"Nina, that's brilliant! You're the best."

"I know," says Nina with a wide smile. "And I got an idea for my own Winter Formal dress out of this too."

"Like I said, win-win," I tell her. I just hope my vision of this dress bringing me, Nina, and Alex together ends up being a winner too.

SEQUIN BOMBER JACKET

FLOWY SILK SKIRT

FITTED JERSEY-STYLE TOP

SPORTY SEQUIN PANT

TANK TOP BODICE

THREE STRIPES AT SIDE SEAM

MESH JERSEY DRESS

BASEBALL SHIRT-INSPIRED Designs

35

"Are you sure you don't mind me helping you today?" my mom asks on Friday afternoon as we sit in my room, waiting for my final Winter Formal client, Jillian Vaughn, to arrive. Normally Alex would be here with me to help organize everything, but she had to stay after school to finish a test.

It might be for the best, I think. Alex is still acting weird about me hanging out with Nina yesterday, and I was a little relieved she had something to do today. All I kept picturing was another argument, and I didn't have the energy to deal with that.

"I don't mind at all," I assure her. "I'm happy you're here."

Just then the doorbell rings, and my mom goes downstairs to get Jillian. To be honest, when Jillian made the appointment, my first instinct was to hand her over to Nina. From what I've seen of Jillian's style, she's a little out there. Plus, she seems to love arguing, even when she's wrong. But, then Nina and I became close, and I felt bad sticking her with Jillian. Plus I figure it's good for me to test myself as a designer, even if it's not always my favorite thing to do.

"Is this where all the magic happens?" Jillian asks from my doorway. She wrinkles her nose. I can't tell if she's trying to be funny, or if she hates my room.

"I'm afraid so," I say. I figure that's a truthful answer either way.

"Well, then," Mom says, clapping her hands together, "let's get started." She takes a seat on the floor and picks up my laptop.

"Do you have any ideas in mind?" I ask Jillian.

"I've heard the other girls talking about how pretty your designs were," Jillian comments.

I smile. Maybe I was wrong about her. "Thank you. Want to look through some of my sketches and see if anything speaks to you?"

I open my sketchpad and hand it over. Jillian quickly flips through the pages. After a moment she hands it back.

"These *are* pretty," she says with a sigh, "but none of them are exactly what I had in mind."

"If you tell me a little about what you're looking for, I can try to create something that matches your vision," I offer.

"I think it would probably just be easier if I drew my ideas. Is that okay?" asks Jillian. She doesn't wait for me to answer before grabbing my sketchbook back and flipping to a clean page.

My mom raises an eyebrow, but I just shrug. I've had to deal with all kinds of personalities while designing for Winter Formal, and I know that won't change in the real world either. I'm trying to be better about just rolling with it. But even so, Jillian makes me a little nervous. She seems so picky.

Less than five minutes later, Jillian hands the sketchbook back. "Done."

My jaw drops when I see the designs. They look like something from a science fiction movie. Each piece is made up of harsh, jutting angles and bright metallic colors. One of the dresses looks like someone wrapped in green aluminum foil.

"I know they're not the same style as your other dresses, but I want a Chloe original without it *looking* like a Chloe original. Does that make sense?" asks Jillian.

"Not really," I say curtly.

My mom clears her throat. "I'm sure there's something Chloe can do that combines some of your favorite ideas with hers," she says.

I fight the urge to roll my eyes. I know my mom is trying to help, but I don't know how to combine any of my vision with Jillian's. I'm not sure if I even *want* to. If I give her exactly what she wants, the result won't be anything I want to take credit for. I'm starting to regret not sending her Nina's way.

Jillian and my mom both look my way, waiting for me to speak, and I force myself to take a deep breath. "Uh . . . yeah. I can try to see if there's a way we can compromise."

I draw a long, fitted dress in an electric blue metallic color. Then I add a leopard-print belt and collar and pair it with blue platforms. The design is different from the more traditional dresses I've done for other clients, but I can live with it.

"Hmmm . . . it's a start," Jillian says, "but it needs more drama. How about adding sequins around the middle and —"

"Sequins will make it really busy," I interrupt before I can stop myself.

"Well, I don't want just sequins," Jillian says shortly. "Feathers too."

"Actual feathers?" I ask.

Jillian nods. "Like this." She takes a gray pencil and adds feathered sleeves that look awesome — for an owl or some other bird.

I study the sketch, trying to find something diplomatic to say, but all I come up with is, "I can't see feathers working."

"Fine," Jillian says shortly. "What about something with bows?"

I perk up. "I like bows. They make great accent pieces."

Jillian shakes her head. "I don't want to play it safe." She takes a bunch of colored pencils and starts sketching.

"That's a lot of colors," says my mom politely, echoing my not-so-polite thoughts.

"Here. This is the one," Jillian says, handing me my sketchpad.

I study the page. This design is even worse than feathered sleeves. The dress is flowing and reaches the floor. But you can barely see it underneath the dozens of huge, multicolored bows Jillian drew all over the dress.

"There's hardly a dress here," I say.

Jillian's Addition

FEATHERED SLEEVES

BOWS!!

FITTED ELECTRIC-BLUE DRESS

Original Look

LEOPARD-PRINT COLLAR & BELT

MORE BOWS!

Jillian looks annoyed. "I thought you were supposed to be good."

"I *am* good!" I snap, raising my voice.

My mom shoots me a warning look, and I take another deep breath, trying to calm down. I remember other dresses I designed that felt out of my element, like the one I did for Sophia Gonzalez. Her ideas were a little out there too. But the difference was that Sophia was nice and actually cared about what I thought.

Jillian rolls her eyes. "Geez. Relax."

"I have another idea," I say through gritted teeth. I start sketching and press too hard on the pencil point. It breaks, and Jillian smirks. "You know what? We don't have to do this. Maybe I'm not the designer for you."

I start to put away my sketchpad. I knew Jillian had the potential to be a tough client, but I was still hoping for a somewhat enjoyable afternoon. Instead, I feel like I'm fighting with someone again — exactly what I wanted to avoid.

"Oh, come on," Jillian whines. "I'm sorry, okay?" She doesn't sound sorry at all. "I'll try to be more open-minded."

"Fine." I pick up another pencil. "But if you don't like this design either, maybe we should just accept that we're not a good match."

I start off with an off-the-shoulder mermaid dress. That alone, with sequins or sparkle, would be gorgeous for someone else. For Jillian, it needs an over-the-top element I can tolerate.

I look through Jillian's sketches. One thing they all have in common is that the dress is almost an afterthought. With that in mind, I cover the dress in horizontal black-and-white stripes. Then I add tiered ruffles to the bottom of the skirt. Thinking of Jillian's feathers, I add ruffles to the sleeves too.

"Thoughts?" I ask, pushing my sketchpad in Jillian's direction.

Jillian studies the design, nodding. "This is more my speed," she says. She doesn't sound thrilled or gush like other girls did when I showed them the final product, but she seems happy enough. "Maybe we can replace the sleeves with long, black gloves?"

"That seems a little tame for you, no?" I know I sound rude, but I don't care. This hasn't gone at all the way I expected it to — I just want it to be over at this point.

Jillian doesn't look offended. "Yeah, you could be right. Either way."

"Great. I'll give this to Mimi. Here's her card. Call and make an appointment for measurements ASAP." I keep my voice all business, afraid I'll sound snippy again.

"Thanks," says Jillian. "It's been real."

"Yeah, real torture," I mutter under my breath when she leaves.

"It could have gone worse," Mom says when we're alone. "Can you at least use this dress in your portfolio?"

"I don't know. Once I design my dress and Alex's I'll have enough, so I probably won't have to."

I study Jillian's design again and feel like throwing something. At least it's finished. And it's not too hideous. But maybe if I have a bad feeling about something in the future, I'll go with my instincts.

36

"Here you go," I tell Mimi when I stop by her store on Saturday. "It's the final dress design. Ta-da!" I take a small bow.

Mimi looks at the drawing I did for Jillian. "It's certainly different," she says. "She came in to be measured right after she left your house yesterday and has already called three times to find out if you dropped off the sketch."

I groan. "That sounds about right."

Mimi doesn't look concerned. "It's life, Chloe. You'll deal with all kinds of people as a designer. Think of it as preparing you for the future."

"Ugh, I know. But between finishing my portfolio and Alex running hot and cold on me, I could use a little less chaos."

Mimi laughs. "And, don't forget, you owe me the designs for you and Alex." She looks at her calendar. "Monday at the latest."

"Right," I say, nodding. "Alex is coming over tomorrow to choose her design, so I can get that to you then."

"She's excited," Mimi tells me. "She came in last night to get measured and save some time."

I want to ask if Alex said anything about me, but I'm not sure how to ask without the question sounding weird. Before I can say anything, Mimi pulls out her tape measure.

"Speaking of measurements, let's get that out of the way for you, too." She instructs me to stand up straight and measures my bust, hips, and waist and writes down the numbers. "Have you thought about what kind of shoes you'll be wearing?"

"For my imaginary dress?" I say with a laugh. "Nope."

Mimi shakes her head. "Fine. I'll leave the length TBD for now then."

"Thanks," I say. "Sorry for putting this off."

"It's okay," Mimi says. "I planned for the possibility. Any ideas at all?"

"Some," I say. "I was thinking about experimenting with a two-piece, like a fitted lace crop-top and a flowing skirt. Or I'm thinking about doing something with a simple silhouette but a bright, bold color. But I haven't

CHLOE'S DRESS Designs

Two-piece designs

CROP TOPS!

LACE

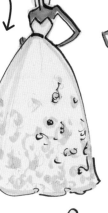

JUMPSUIT

STRAPLESS

TULLE OVERLAY

Bold Color Designs

really narrowed it down too much. I've barely started sketching."

"Let's hope you didn't use up all your design creativity on the other girls," Mimi says with a wink.

I know she's kidding, but that's not even a possibility I want to think about. I look around the store to talk about something else. That's when I spot some familiar-looking designs in the back. "Can I look at those?" I ask.

"Of course!" Mimi says. "Those are the dresses I've finished so far. Nina's designs are there, too, and you haven't seen any of those."

"That's right!" I make a beeline to the back of the store. No matter how many times I sketch something, there's always this excitement and tingly feeling I get when I see the finished product. I'm always amazed when my drawings come to life.

"Pretty wonderful, aren't they?" Mimi says from beside me.

"*You're* wonderful," I say. "I worried if every girl's idea could work, but you made sure every detail is just perfect."

"Thank you, honey," says Mimi.

"Where are Nina's designs?" I ask.

"Most of them are here," says Mimi, moving some dresses from the back of the rack to the front.

"Is the dress Nina is wearing here too?" I ask, trying to sound casual.

Mimi laughs. "Nice try, Chloe. That one is tucked safely away. She wants it to be a surprise."

I smile, not surprised to hear that. "Hey, you can't fault a girl for trying, right?"

I sort through the designs. They all have Nina's signature, feminine touch. I stop at a sea-green gown with a strapless neckline and floor-length, A-line skirt. The skirt is tulle with layers of lace, and rhinestones decorate the waist. "This is beautiful."

"They all are. It's been a pleasure doing these dresses for you girls. Brought me back to my high school days," Mimi says with a smile. She plucks a dress from the back of the line. "You have to see this one."

"Oooh," I whisper as I run my hand over the soft chiffon fabric of the long mermaid-style dress. "I love the crystal beading."

"Yes, that was a lovely touch," says Mimi.

Just then a short, light-blue dress catches my eye. The tulle skirt falls above the knee, and beading covers the neckline and waist. It reminds me of the princess-themed dresses I designed for some of my clients. I like that Nina and I have some of the same ideas. It's another moment that shows me we're not that different.

NINA'S DRESS *Designs*

MERMAID SILHOUETTE

LOW BACK

TINY BOW BELT

SWEETHEART BODICE

CRYSTAL BEADED CHIFFON

RHINESTONES & CRYSTALS

TULLE SKIRT

"I'm really looking forward to seeing Alex's design tomorrow," Mimi says as we make our way back to the front of the store. She stops at the checkout counter and looks in her planner. "I know I told you Monday is the latest, but you'd make my life much easier if you got me your design tomorrow, too. Is that doable at all?"

"I do have some ideas, so it's not like I'll be starting from scratch," I say, thinking out loud. I also have no plans tonight. That's what happens when your best friend is mad at you.

"It doesn't have to be perfect," says Mimi. "Even a rough sketch, with you talking me through the design, will work. I don't want to rush."

I know what it's like to be in a time crunch and feel Mimi's worry. "I'll bring it tomorrow with Alex's. I'm really hoping she likes her dress. Nina helped me brainstorm," I confess.

Mimi's face lights up. "That was a terrific idea," she says.

"You really think so?" I ask. "She and Alex don't get along well."

Mimi nods knowingly. "All the more reason this was the right thing to do. Maybe it'll help bring them together a bit. And it never hurts to have a fresh perspective — and a fresh set of eyes — when designing."

I have a feeling Alex probably confided in Mimi. Like me, it seems Mimi thinks including Nina in Alex's dress design could end their feud. This makes me feel better about my idea. "Here's hoping," I say.

37

"You didn't tell me *she'd* be here!" Alex complains the next afternoon when she walks into my room to see her Winter Formal dress designs — and spots Nina.

Nina bristles. "Lovely to see you too," she says through clenched teeth. She turns to me. "See? I told you."

Alex stomps her foot. "*You* told her? Like I'm the immature one."

Alex *is* being the immature one, but I'm not going to point that out — it would just derail my plan even further.

"Guys, please," I beg. "Alex, Nina is here because she helped me brainstorm options for your dress. Nina, Alex was just surprised to see you but could have handled it better." I nudge Alex. "Right?"

Alex glares at me, but I stare right back. "Right," she finally mumbles.

"Awesome," I say, clapping my hands. "I can feel the love in the room already."

Alex sits down on the floor beside me, and Nina fans out pages of designs. There's the dress with the top that looks like a fitted T-shirt, a couple two-piece options in a variety of colors, and the bathing-suit inspired dress in the scuba material.

Alex starts with a two-piece dress. The fitted lace crop top is light blue and has a halter neckline. The long, full skirt is made of taffeta and features a fun floral pattern.

"This is really pretty," says Alex. "And surprisingly, I love the floral pattern. It's nothing I'd normally wear, but it's really pretty."

"Two-pieces are really in right now," Nina comments. "Some of my designs for Winter Formal use elements of this one."

"I stopped by Mimi's yesterday, and saw your dresses," I mention casually. "We actually share a few of the same ideas."

Nina's face looks panicked. "You saw my dresses? Like all of them?"

I realize why she's so worried. "Not the design for your dress. Mimi wouldn't let me."

Nina looks relieved. "It's not like I *care* if you see my work. I just wanted my dress to be a surprise."

"Right. I totally get that. Mine will be a surprise too. Once I finish it, that is."

Alex puts the first sketch to the side, and looks at my other sports-inspired dresses. "I like the idea of s sporty dress, but I want something different than the everyday me, you know?" she says gently, searching my face to see if I'm offended.

"I understand. I tried to combine both worlds with this dress," I say, handing her a drawing, "but I think last year's Alex would have liked this more."

Alex studies the design of a classic taffeta ball gown skirt, paired with a fitted bodice with two stripes on the side seams. It's fancier than the first sketch I showed Nina a few days ago, but I know it's still not exactly what Alex is looking for.

Nina seems to sense that too and hands Alex the sketch of the scuba dress, which now shines in a playful, but still elegant, floral pattern.

Alex's face lights up. "Oh wow. This. Definitely this."

Seeing her so happy makes me happy. Nina smiles widely too.

I clear my throat. "Nina was actually the inspiration for this design. She's the one who suggested I play with the scuba material that I used for some of my FIDM sketches and use that for your dress."

Alex takes her eyes off the design and looks at Nina. She swallows, like she needs help getting the words out. "Thank you, Nina."

Nina collapses on my floor. "*Thank you?*" she echoes. "The world is ending! It's the apocalypse!"

I expect Alex to say something nasty, but to my surprise, she bursts out laughing. "Must be," she says with a shrug.

Another crisis averted, I bring the discussion back to the dress. "So like I said, this will be in a scuba material, like what I used in my portfolio designs. It's body-con, but the material is softer and thicker and will let you move around easily."

"Perfect. I do like to be comfortable." Alex stares at the dress, like the sketch will disappear.

"I also added a sweetheart neckline and decided to go with a floral print to make it softer and more feminine," I tell her.

"I love the purple heels with it too," says Alex. "It's perfect. You're the best," She finally tears herself away from the picture to give me a hug. She's smiling when she pulls back, but her face gets apprehensive as she looks at Nina.

"Don't even think about it!" says Nina, holding out her arms in defense. "Baby steps. There will be no hugging between us yet."

ALEX'S FINAL DRESS *Design*

BRAIDED HAIR CROWN

STRAPLESS TO SHOW A TOUCH OF SKIN

MULTICOLOR FLORAL PATTERN

FORMFITTING

Perfect Style!

STRAPPY PURPLE HEELS

"Phew," says Alex, pretending to wipe sweat from her brow. "I really do appreciate this, Chloe. I know I haven't been the easiest person to deal with lately."

I'm surprised Alex is opening herself up like this with Nina here, but it shows me we can finally move on. It's the perfect moment to show her my portfolio project of her evolving styles.

"I have another surprise for you," I say. "I've been using you as inspiration for my college applications."

Alex looks nervous. "Inspiration for what, exactly?"

"Nothing bad, silly!" I take out my sketches of Alex's outfits — past and present — and show them to her.

Alex's eyes grow wide as she examines the drawings. She looks at each one slowly and carefully. When she's done, she goes back to the first and looks at them all again.

"Chloe," she whispers. "I don't know what to say. These are fantastic, and you choosing *my* style for your portfolio. I just . . ." She stops talking and gives me another big hug. "I'm lucky to have you as a friend."

"Back at you," I say.

I peek at Nina from the corner of my eye and see her absently looking at all my sketches. I've spent enough time with her to know she's uncomfortable and not sure of her place here. The last thing I want is for Nina to feel left out now.

"Do you both have to be home for dinner?" I ask impulsively.

Alex and Nina shake their heads.

"My mom is working late," Nina says.

"And we're having leftover casserole," Alex adds, wrinkling her nose.

"Great!" I say. "Let's have dinner together. I have to take this to Mimi, but after that we can order in and hang out."

Nina unzips her backpack and takes out the most recent issue of a fashion magazine I love. "Maybe after we eat, we can look through this and grade the outfits," she says shyly.

I glance over at Alex. She looks like she's struggling with what to say. "That's a great idea," she finally manages.

I call Mimi and tell her I'll be over soon to drop off the sketch for Alex's dress — along with the rough idea for mine, which I finalized last night. After I hang up, I peek at Alex and Nina, who are busy thumbing through the magazines together. I realize the two of them may never be super close, but they're both trying. That's all I can ask for.

38

Two days later, I'm sitting on my floor, portfolio sketches sorted into neat piles by college. They're finished, for the most part, but I've added a few swimsuits to my seasonal designs for FIDM, one more Lola James piece for FIT, and my formal dress design and Alex's.

My phone rings, and I see *Jake* flash across the screen. I quickly answer the call. "Hey!" I practically sing into the phone.

"Hey, yourself," Jake replies, and I can tell by his voice that he's smiling. "I can't believe I get to see you this weekend."

"I know!" I say. "I'm trying not to think about that, though."

There's a beat of silence before Jake says, "Really?"

"Not because I don't *want* to see you!" I quickly reassure him. "I just meant I'm trying not to think about that because I'm finishing up my college applications, and if I start daydreaming about this weekend and Winter Formal and you being here for the holidays, I know I'll procrastinate."

"College stress. That's better," Jake teases. "I thought maybe you'd changed your mind about me coming."

"Never," I say. "In fact, I wish you could be here right now to help me finish all of this."

"I couldn't do that even if I were there," says Jake, "but I appreciate the vote of confidence."

"You mean you don't have magic fairy dust?" I pout. "I underestimated you."

"Ouch," he says. "I can send super productive vibes. How's that?"

"It will do." I so miss our banter and him.

"Can you tell me about your dress?" Jake asks, changing the subject. "I want to wear a matching tie."

"My dress is a secret. I want you to see me and be dazzled."

"I'll be dazzled either way," he says. "It's just that I'm staring at my new suit and need to know how to spice it up. How about the color?"

"I can do color because that's really not giving anything away — red," I say.

"Red tie, it is," Jake says.

I giggle as I imagine Jake sorting through racks of ties to find the perfect shade.

"You'd make a good spy," he says. "Well, I'll let you get back to your college stuff. I won't try to make you divulge more dress secrets."

"Ugh, good point," I agree. "I should put my applications out of their misery. See you soon!"

"Sooner than soon," says Jake.

After we hang up, I can't stop smiling. Then, I look at the piles on my floor, and my smile disappears. I was kind of hoping the applications would miraculously finish themselves while I was on the phone. No such luck.

This is the home stretch, Chloe, I tell myself. *You can do it!*

I start with my pop star designs and add definition to another of Lola's lounging around outfits — skinny jeans, a plaid shirt, and brown ankle boots. Then, I move on to one of Alex's pieces. Her style evolution has been my favorite part of working on my portfolio.

I already added the final design — Alex's Winter Formal dress — to the mix, but I wanted to highlight the prints in a casual style I sketched. I define a silk camisole

CHLOE'S PORTFOLIO *Designs*

ALEX'S LOOK!

PLAID SHIRT

SKINNY STRAP TANK TOP

ROLLED SLEEVE CUFFS

FLORAL PANTS

ANKLE BOOTS

ROLLED SKINNY JEANS

LOLA JAMES LOOK!

BLACK FLATS

and outline white flowers on the black pants. Then, I pair the piece with black flats. Done!

It's a relief for my portfolios to be nearly finished, but I've also learned so much in this process. If it weren't for this assignment, I never would have gotten the idea for Alex's dress or stretched my designing ability. These applications showed me how to expand on what I know. It's a skill I'll keep working on wherever I end up going to college.

I pick up a sketch of a bathing suit — a two-piece with a bandeau-style top that's outlined in thick black stitching. The design on the high-waisted briefs features different-sized shapes in blue, black, yellow, and red outlined in white.

I left this one for today because it required a lot of precise coloring, and I didn't want to get bogged down in details while I had other sketches to complete. Now that the bathing suit is finished, I get to work transforming the design into something that can be worn away from the beach. I sketch a sweater dress in a similar style, adding tall black boots and further defining the shape and color.

My mom walks into my room just as I finish. "How's it going?" she asks.

I throw my hands up in the air victoriously and let out a sigh of relief. "I'm done!"

Mom swoops in and gives me a big hug. "Oh, honey, I'm so proud of you. We need to celebrate!"

"Maybe we should hold off on the celebration. I haven't sent the applications in yet."

Mom waves her hand, dismissing my comment. "You have two weeks until deadline. I know you wanted to finish before holiday vacation, and you did it. Now, give yourself a break — at least until Winter Formal this weekend. Just enjoy yourself."

"I just hope I didn't forget how," I say.

My mom rolls her eyes. "My daughter the drama queen. Let's go tell your dad and plan a celebratory dinner. We can go to that new restaurant you've been begging us to try."

"That would be terrific. Thank you! I just want to put everything away first."

Mom nods, and after one final hug, she heads back downstairs. Once she's gone, I move all the sketches from my floor to my desk. That makes everything more official somehow. I like seeing my floor all clean and uncluttered. It's been months since it's been free of college stuff. The biggest decision — where I'll get in and where to actually enroll — is still ahead of me, but for now it's time to have some fun!

MONDRIAN-INSPIRED DRESS

COLOR-BLOCKED PATTERN

SWIMSUIT PORTFOLIO *Designs*

MOD SUNGLASSES

BANDEAU TOP

THIGH-HIGH BOOTS

SQUARE, BLOCKED PATTERN

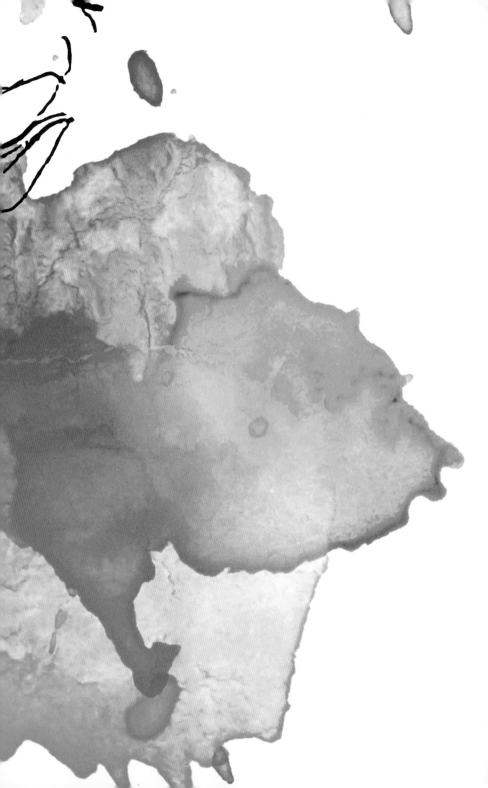

The doorbell rings, and my first thought is to run to the door, but I'm still getting ready. Alex's and Nina's voices float up the stairs, and a moment later, I hear Jake and Dan too. Now I really need to hurry.

I put a gold clip in my hair and check myself out in the mirror one last time. The dress I ended up creating is an A-line silhouette with a full skirt and a strapless bodice in a bright, bold red. The long, floor-length hem just brushes the ground, and the bustier-style bodice is accentuated with a black ribbon and bow detail at the waist. To break up the bright color, I also added a large, abstract feather design on the skirt.

I twirl in front of the mirror, and the dress moves with me. A year ago, I would have never worn this. I would have chosen something in all black or another neutral, solid color. My designs — and my personal style — have come a long way.

"Chloe, stop showing off to the mirror, and come down!" Alex shouts from the first floor. She knows me so well.

I grab my clutch and realize my hand is shaking. Why am I so nervous? I hold onto the banister as I make my way down the stairs and into the living room, worried I'll trip over my feet and come crashing to the floor. That would put a damper on the night's events for sure. I wrap my fingers tighter around the railing.

"Hey, everyone," I say when I step into the living room.

"You look amazing!" Alex exclaims. She looks absolutely stunning in her fun, floral-print dress. Her hair is pulled back slightly with a braid across her forehead, and the rest of her hair falls in soft waves past her shoulders.

"You do," Nina agrees. "I love that color. And the feather is such a unique touch."

I take in Nina's dress. "Your dress is so elegant," I gush. She's wearing a floor-length strapless dress in mint with gold embroidery across the bodice and a gold belt at the waist.

"Thank you," says Nina, blushing. "I worked really hard on it."

"The gold details are stunning," Alex adds.

Jake clears his throat. "Not to interrupt the love fest, but can I take a look at my date?" he asks.

Everyone laughs, and I blush. I want to run up to him and hug him, but that would be a little awkward with everyone watching.

Jake walks up to me and takes my hands. "You look beautiful," he whispers.

My cheeks redden some more. "Thank you," I reply. "I like the red tie. The red pocket square is a nice touch too."

"Do you think we can take some photographs of you dazzling people?" Dad asks.

"Let's take them outside," Mom suggests. "You all look fantastic, and that way we can take advantage of the natural light."

Everyone agrees and heads for the front door. Jake squeezes my hand as we go. "I'm so glad I can be here with you," he whispers.

"Me too," I agree, squeezing his hand in return. "There's no one else I'd rather be with."

* * *

"Aaah!" Jada squeals as our group makes its way to our shared table thirty minutes later. "You all look so fabulous!"

"So do you," I say. Nina designed Jada's dress, and the long, white off-the-shoulder gown looks beautiful on Jada's lean frame and against her dark skin. A silver clasp decorates the left shoulder strap.

Jada puts an arm around Nina. "I have this girl to thank," she says.

"My pleasure," says Nina, smiling. She looks so relaxed and happy.

I glance around, taking in our little group. Everyone is excited and thrilled to be here. It's such a change from the start of the year, when we were all stressing about college applications. I can't believe how quickly the time has gone.

"Wait!" I say, realizing something. "Where's Mia?"

"Late, as usual," a voice says from behind me. I turn and see Mia approaching.

"*Fashionably* late at least," Jada says, laughing.

"That's for sure," says Mia. She has a new razor edge haircut, and a streak of blue across her bangs. "You all love my Chloe original?"

"Definitely," says Alex. "It's very you." The dress I designed for Mia is a cream two-piece with a sheer, mesh skirt with a ribbon hem. The midriff-baring bodice is decorated with crystal beading.

"I'm so glad we can be here together," I say. It's like the best of both worlds having all my friends *and* Jake here. If only there was a college near both him and Alex. That'd make my life a lot easier.

"You're saying that like it's the last time," says Jada, frowning.

"Close enough," mumbles Alex.

Mia rolls her eyes. "Here we go. Since when did Alex become Miss Glass-Half-Empty?"

"I'm not half-empty," Alex argues. "It's just sad to think about — and a little overwhelming. This is the last time we'll all be together at a winter dance like this."

Everyone seems to realize how right she is at the same time, and we all fall silent.

"You girls are always too serious," Dan says, breaking the somber mood. "We have a whole second semester together. And this is supposed to be a dance — a party! It's like you all *want* something to be upset about."

I glare at Dan, as do the rest of the girls, but if I'm being honest, he's not totally wrong. But, it's not that we *want* to be upset. It's hard to explain. It's more like sometimes, at least for me, when everything is going super well, I think about what would happen if they weren't. Like now.

Everything is awesome, but I know in a few months we'll be graduating. It's hard to forget that.

"Well," Jake interjects, "I think it's more that the girls are being realistic, and you, sir, like to live in the moment."

Dan snorts. "Life's better that way."

Just then there's crackling on the stage, and one of the chaperones, Mrs. Reed, takes the mic. "Thank you all for coming today," she says. "We're going to do things a little differently for this dance, and announce our Winter King and Queen at the start of the festivities. So if you'll all take your seats, we have some winners to announce."

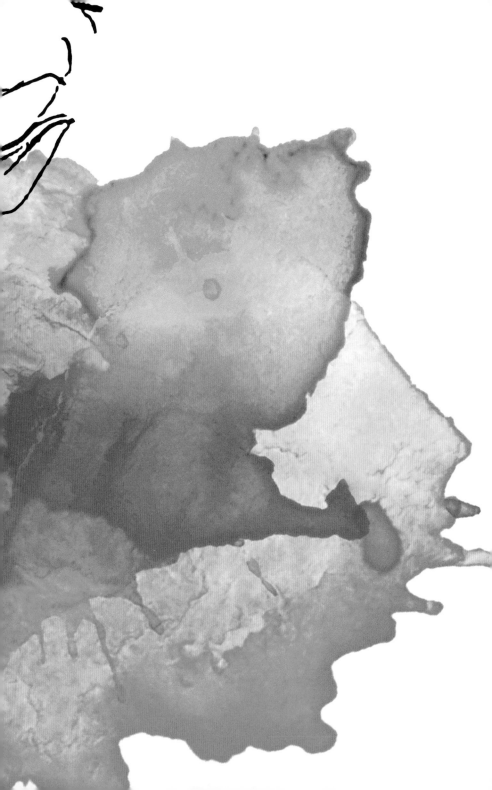

There's an excited buzz around the room, and everyone seems to stand a little straighter. I had honestly totally forgotten about there being a king and queen at the Winter Formal. I've been so busy designing dresses for the dance that the rest of the logistics sort of slipped my mind. I didn't even remember to vote!

Mrs. Reed takes a golden envelope from her pocket, not wasting any time. "This year's Winter Formal King and Queen are . . ." She motions for the band to do a drum roll. "Daniel Castro and Alexis McGill!"

We all gasp with excitement. Alex looks stunned as people around us congratulate her.

"Come on!" Dan calls, pulling Alex to the stage.

"Remember what she was like when you first met her at that craft fair last year?" I say to Jake, shouting over the noise.

Jake nods and laughs. "That Alex would have run out the door."

"And would have asked if there was a way to make sweatpants into a formal dress," I add, laughing.

"Speech!" shouts Jada, and others in the room pick up the chant.

Dan gives the mic to Alex. "My queen is better with words than yours truly," he says.

Alex tries to push the mic away, but then Mia starts a cheer of "Alex, Alex, Alex!" and she reluctantly takes the mic.

"Um, thank you all so much," Alex begins. "I never, ever thought I'd be up here, and in such a fancy dress! I have my best friend Chloe to thank for that. Let's give her a hand."

My face is burning as everyone claps and shouts my name.

"And, of course, the other star of the night is Nina," Alex continues, smiling widely. "Many of you are wearing her designs too. Take a bow, Nina."

Nina looks a little embarrassed, but she grins as everyone cheers and claps.

"What's next on the design to-do list now that Winter Formal is done?" asks Mia, turning to Nina and me, as Alex finishes her speech.

Jada snaps her fingers. "Prom, of course."

"First dibs!" they both say.

I look wearily at Nina, and she gives me the same look back. "At least we won't have to worry about college applications by then," she says.

"Just finals and graduation," I say, groaning. "No big deal."

Nina winks. "Piece of cake."

"You can design together," Jake suggests.

"Design what?" Alex asks, finally rejoining us. The silver crown sparkles on her head.

"The prom dresses," says Jake.

"Oooh, dibs!" Alex exclaims.

Mia laughs. "Already called it," she says. "So did Jada. You're third, though."

Thankfully, before anyone else can rope me into designing another dress, the band plays my favorite song, and Jake takes my hand. "Can I collect on the dance you promised me?" he asks.

"Of course," I say, walking with him to the dance floor.

* * *

That night, after Jake drives me home, we sit on my porch swing. The last time I was here, I was so nervous about even mentioning Winter Formal to him. Funny how things can change.

"Did you have fun?" I ask him.

"I always have fun with you," Jake says. "It was nice to meet more of your friends too."

"They thought you were great."

"Glad I passed the test," he replies with a smile.

"Haha. Just stating a fact. There was no test," I say.

Jake takes my hand. "I wish we could hang out more, but my dad is excited about having me home for the holidays. He made all these plans for us, starting tomorrow."

I'm bummed but try to stay upbeat. "We'll keep talking, texting, and emailing, like we always do."

"And there's prom," Jake adds quickly. "Assuming you have time to go in between all the dresses you'll apparently be designing. And assuming you plan on asking me, that is."

I rub my chin, pretending to think about it. "Yeah, you make the cut." We sit quietly for a few minutes, and then I add, "For now, I'd like to borrow Dan's idea."

"What's that?" asks Jake.

"To not think about the future," I say.

Jake gives me a hug. "That Dan is a smart guy."

For the next few minutes, for a change, I focus only on the present.

41

"I can't believe Mimi invited us to her holiday party this year!" Mia exclaims as we wait for Mimi to open the door.

The invite was very last minute, which is very Mimi. Two days after Winter Formal, she called me and said she loved working with us this year and was going to miss us and would love it if we came to her party. A week later, here we are.

"Do you think we'll see any movie stars?" Jada asks. "I've lived in California since the summer and still haven't seen one!"

I can't help but laugh. Jada could certainly pass for a movie star in a black silk tank, paired with loose-fitting gold pants and black heels. It's easy to imagine her look at a post-Oscars party. But the likelihood of us seeing an *actual* celebrity in Santa Cruz? Slim to none.

I pat her hand. "I've lived here my whole life and still haven't seen one. Don't get your hopes up. I bet Mimi has famous friends, but probably old-school famous."

"It would still be cool to hear their stories," says Nina. "I love when Mimi tells us about her days in Hollywood."

As if she heard her name, Mimi chooses that moment to open the door. "Welcome," she says, ushering us inside and giving all of us hugs. She's wearing a floor-length velvet gown sewn with silver embroidery and a draped neckline.

We step into Mimi's marble-floored foyer. Holiday decorations are displayed at the entryway. There are guests in fancy dresses chatting on the staircase leading upstairs and standing in the huge living room sprawled out in front of us. Past the living room's glass doors, I spot even more guests milling about in Mimi's garden. There must be more than one hundred people here!

"Didn't you say this would be a small party?" I say.

"Oh, darling," says Mimi, "back in the day this would be called an intimate gathering."

"Your home is beautiful," says Nina. "I might be underdressed." Nina looks party-ready in a gold sequined cocktail dress with a black ribbon tied around the waist.

Mimi shakes her head. "Nonsense. You fit right in."

I agree with Mimi, but I get what Nina means. Mimi's home is so impressive, I feel like I should be wearing something more red-carpet ready. However, I feel confident in today's outfit — even though I almost chickened out and didn't wear it. It's a strapless jumpsuit with a deep V-neck in bright fuchsia. It's a very un-Chloe color, but the New Year will be here in less than a week, and I'm starting it off early and with a bang.

"Enjoy yourselves and mingle," says Mimi with a small wave. "Food will be out shortly. Until then, enjoy the hors d'oeuvres."

My friends and I mill around together, collecting appetizers on our plates. "I'm so glad we're here together," I say. "I'd be a little intimidated to be here alone."

We walk to a far corner of the room, where an empty sofa awaits. Alex sits on its arm, glass in one hand and white, feathered clutch in the other. Her strappy V-neck camisole and sequin pants remind me of an outfit I've seen on Lola James in a fashion magazine. "I could get used to this," she says, taking a sip of her juice.

"Not me," I say. "I'll be the mysterious name *behind* the label."

"That works for me," says Nina. "I don't need you stealing my spotlight." She pretends to elbow me out of the way.

HOLIDAY PARTY *Designs*

DRAPED NECKLINE

NINA'S OUTFIT

SILK TANK TOP

GOLD PANTS

BOW BELT

GOLD SEQUINS

JADA'S OUTFIT

MIMI'S OUTFIT

HOLIDAY PARTY *Designs*

CHLOE'S OUTFIT

SILK CAMISOLE

FEATHER CLUTCH

STRAPLESS BODICE

SEQUIN PANTS

SKINNY PANTS

FUCHSIA JUMPSUIT

ALEX'S OUTFIT

"And we return to the big question," says Mia, adjusting her fitted sparkly dress and black tights. "Will this label be in Cali or New York?"

Jada groans. "We're having a good time. Why bring that up?"

"Yeah," says Alex. "I'm pulling a Dan and living in the now."

Mia holds up her hands surrender style. "It was just a question. Sheesh."

My eyes twinkle. "Well, if we're talking strictly about my future imaginary label, won't it be everywhere? New York, Paris, California, Milan . . ."

Nina gives me a high-five. "Good answer, Chloe." She looks around the room, pulls out her phone, and types something into it. "That woman's gown just gave me an idea for a prom dress design."

Alex groans. "Don't you ever rest?"

Nina shrugs. "Sketching and creating makes me happiest, and when I get an idea I need to jot something down immediately so I don't forget."

"Chloe's the same way," says Alex, smiling. She looks around the room and nods at someone. "That one."

"What?" I ask, confused.

"That knee-length strapless dress will be my prom dress inspiration. Write it down, Chloe," Alex says, winking.

I laugh and make a note in my phone.

"This is a good game," Mia says. She glances at the patio doors. "I pick the woman with the spiky pink hair. I love that long blue gown. The color is so fun and vibrant."

We look around the room, picking out more dress inspiration. This party is exactly what I needed. Tomorrow, Nina and I have plans to mail our applications together since they have the same deadline. It was actually Alex's idea; she's doing the same thing with Mia in January.

"Let's make a toast," says Alex.

We all raise our glasses of juice and soda.

"To good friends," Nina begins.

"To good times," Jada says.

"To new friends," says Alex, glancing at Nina.

"To new experiences," Mia adds.

"And to always finding a way to get together, no matter how far away we all go," I finish.

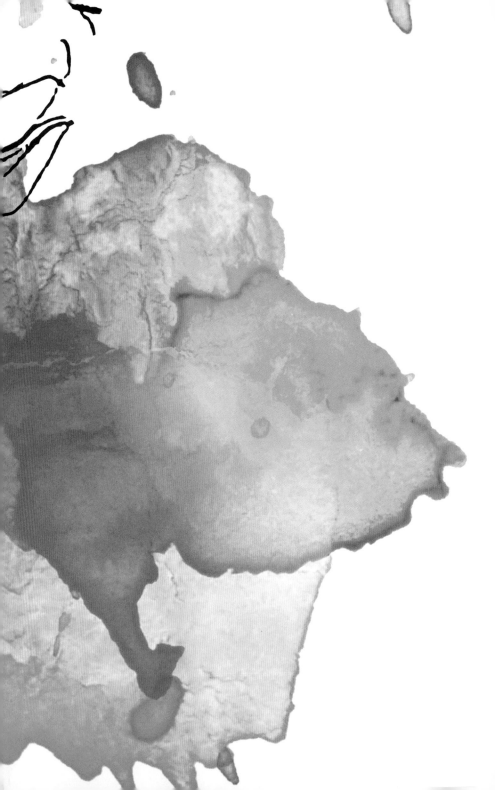

"You do realize how dorky we are, right?" Nina says the next day. We're sitting at Nina's kitchen table, laptops open and our portfolio requirements ready to be uploaded.

"Sending our applications at the same time is not that weird," I argue.

"No, but dressing up to do it is."

"That was all *your* idea!" I say, laughing.

Nina blushes. "I know, but you went along with it."

"That's because I'm dorky too. Besides, it's not like we're in our Winter Formal dresses or anything."

Nina's idea was to make this sending of our applications totally college-themed and to wear something we might wear the first day of classes. Since we're applying to schools in California and New York, we flipped a coin to see who got which style. Nina got Cali, and I got New York.

I feel a little silly sitting in Nina's kitchen in a black leather skirt, loose white blouse, and black ankle boots, but Nina's outfit — a denim jacket over a lilac-colored dress with flower print — isn't necessarily typical hanging around the house attire either.

"It does make this a little more fun, doesn't it?" asks Nina.

"Yep," I say, pulling up the FIDM website, "but I'm still nervous."

"Good," says Nina. "I thought it was just me. I mean, why are we so nervous? It's not like we're going to find out if we got in immediately."

"Exactly," I say. "And it's not like something big happens once we hit send."

Nina moves her mouse absently. She sighs. "This is going to sound dumb, but it's almost a letdown finally submitting everything."

"What do you mean?"

Nina thinks about what she's trying to say. "I've worked on these designs and applications for so long; it's *all* I've done for months. Once I send everything in, I won't know what to do with myself!"

I laugh. "I know exactly what you mean. I kind of feel the same way, but then I remind myself that I can have a life again, and I feel better."

Nina grins. "A life that *doesn't* involve being holed up in my room working on my portfolio?" she jokes. "What's that like?"

I laugh. "I'll let you know when I find out." I take a deep breath. "We should probably get started. I have the FIDM site ready."

Nina pulls up the site on her laptop, and we both start attaching our documents and drawings, which we've already scanned so we have electronic versions. I start with my series on Alex's evolving style. It's like a trip down memory lane for me. It's been fun remembering Alex's old looks and how they've changed.

When I'm done, I move on to the bathing suit line. Who would've thought that when I started creating these, I'd be inspired to create Alex's Winter Formal dress too?

"How's it going?" asks Nina.

"Almost ready to hit send on all my FIDM stuff," I say. "You?"

Nina checks something in her notes and then types on her laptop. "Same."

"Let's do it," I say. "One."

"Two," says Nina.

PORTFOLIO:
SWIMSUIT
Designs

STYLE
EVOLUTION
Designs

PORTFOLIO:
ALEX'S STYLE
Designs

"Three," I say. We hit our buttons at the same time, and it's done. The first application is off and floating in cyberspace.

"Is it weird I got a rush out of that?" asks Nina.

"We're sitting here in back-to-school outfits," I say. "This entire day is weird."

"True," Nina says, laughing. "Parsons next?"

"Why not?" I gather the Parsons requirements. I admire all the formal dresses I designed for the themed clothing line. When I started putting the designs side-by-side for my portfolio, it was cool to see the range in dress styles and colors. I like seeing bits of myself in each of them.

"Ready?" asks Nina, her mouse hovering over the send button once more.

I nod, and we count down again before hitting send.

"One left," I say. Excited, I pull up my pop star designs for FIT. Nina does the same.

"These Diana Gardo styles were probably my favorite to draw," Nina comments. She looks away from her laptop and sits back in her chair. "Being able to stretch my designing skills was what I liked best about this whole process. If I hadn't been required to create that fall line or play with edgy styles like I did for Diana's look, I would have never known I could design out of my comfort zone. Apparently, there's a world beyond florals and pastels." She laughs.

PORTFOLIO:
DRESS
Designs

PORTFOLIO:
POP STAR
Designs

"That's what I loved best, too," I say. "It was beyond stressful, but now that I'm done, I'm less scared to try out new design elements."

"It's good prep for college no matter where we end up," Nina adds. "All the schools have high expectations. We might as well start getting used to it."

"Right," I agree. "Let's get this done, so we can make the most of the time we have to chill out. Knowing what's ahead for us makes me even more determined to relax now."

"True," says Nina. "Are we counting down again?"

"How else can we make sure we send them at the exact same time?" I ask, grinning.

"I'm just glad no one's recording this. This is dorkiness at its finest."

"One," I say.

"Two," says Nina.

"Three."

We hit send one last time and then sit back. After months of stress and hard work, all three applications — FIT, FIDM, and Parsons — are officially done and sent. All that's left to do now is wait.

It's March, and I'm sitting on my living room floor, three thick envelopes at my feet.

"This is the big moment, huh?" asks my mom.

"Do you want privacy while you open them?" asks Dad.

"Definitely not," I say shakily.

"Which one first?" Mom asks.

"Let's go with FIDM," I say. I run my nail under the envelope seal, opening it carefully so I don't rip anything important. I quickly scan the first page of the packet, but it's the first word — CONGRATULATIONS — that's key.

"I got in," I whisper.

My parents hug me, and I give them the packet to read for themselves in case I imagined it.

"We're so proud of you, honey," my dad says.

"Parsons next?" I ask. I open it quickly, less carefully than the first. This time I stop reading at the first word. "I got in here, too!" I shout.

"I had no doubt," Mom says proudly.

"Shall we make it three for three?" asks Dad.

Unable to contain my excitement, I tear open FIT's envelope. I rip the first page, but only the heading — another CONGRATULATIONS.

"Oh my gosh. I can't believe this!" I shout.

"I can," Mom says, voice wobbly. She swallows and wipes at her eyes before speaking. "You're a determined young lady, Chloe. You worked so hard to get here, and all that is paying off."

"Now that it's official," Dad says, "you'll have to make a choice."

"I know." I stare at the three packets. I think about the fun I had with my friends the past few months. I think about Jake in New York.

"And?" Mom asks.

"I've pretty much decided," I admit. "But I want to think about it a little more."

"You have until May," Dad points out. "That's plenty of time."

"Plenty of time to obsess," Mom says, laughing.

I laugh too, but for once I'm not freaking out. "That's the thing," I say. "I don't feel like that anymore. I'll be okay no matter where I go. Each school and city has its pros and cons."

"Wow," says my dad. "I'm impressed with this new, evolved Chloe."

"Does this mean you'll no longer be our little worrier?" Mom asks.

"Let's not get crazy," I say with a laugh. "We all know I haven't gotten a totally new personality. I'm sure I'll still look at everything from a hundred different angles and wonder if I made the right decision. But as far as this college thing goes, I guess I've made peace with it."

"It probably helps that all those things you were worrying about at once are done," Mom says. She counts off on her fingers. "Finishing your portfolio, designing the Winter Formal dresses, worrying about whether or not you'd get in at all . . . put that all together with deciding where to go, and it became this Mt. Everest of decisions."

I nod slowly. "Probably. I learned a lot from all of it, though. But that doesn't mean I'm not relieved it's all done," I add with a laugh.

"Very true," says Dad.

"Well, I believe you have some phone calls to make," Mom says. "I'm sure you want to share the good news."

I nod. A few months ago, I would have been nervous to call Jake and Alex. I would have worried about their reactions, but now I know they'll be happy for me no matter what. We each have our own journey, and part of the excitement is in how we'll all get there.

The Author

Margaret Gurevich has wanted to be a writer since second grade and has written for many magazines, including *Girls' Life*, *SELF*, and *Ladies' Home Journal*. Her first young adult novel, *Inconvenient*, was a Sydney Taylor Notable Book for Teens, and her second novel, *Pieces of Us*, garnered positive reviews from *Kirkus*, *VOYA*, and *Publishers Weekly*, which called it "painfully believable." When not writing, Margaret enjoys hiking, cooking, reading, watching too much television, and spending time with her husband and son.

The Illustrator

Brooke Hagel is a fashion illustrator based in New York City. While studying fashion design at the Fashion Institute of Technology, she began her career as an intern, working in the wardrobe department of *Sex and the City*, the design studios of Cynthia Rowley, and the production offices of *Saturday Night Live*. After graduating, Brooke began designing and styling for Hearst Magazines, contributing to *Harper's Bazaar*, *House Beautiful*, *Seventeen*, and *Esquire*. Brooke is now a successful illustrator with clients including *Vogue*, *Teen Vogue*, *InStyle*, Dior, Brian Atwood, Hugo Boss, Barbie, Gap, and Neutrogena.

MEASURE TWICE, CUT ONCE
OR YOU WON'T

Make the

Cut